This book should be returned to any branch of the
Lancashire County Library on or before the date shown

1 6 OCT 2018

a daring rescue mission

Cou LANCASHIRE COUNTY LIBRARY my?

OXFORD
UNIVERSITY PRESS

Great Clarendon Street, Oxford OX2 6DP

Oxford University Press is a department of the University of Oxford.
It furthers the University's objective of excellence in research, scholarship,
and education by publishing worldwide. Oxford is a registered trade mark of
Oxford University Press in the UK and in certain other countries

British Library Cataloguing in Publication Data
Data available
ISBN: 978-0-19-274703-7
1 3 5 7 9 10 8 6 4 2
Printed in Great Britain
Paper used in the production of this book is a natural,
recyclable product made from wood grown in sustainable forests.
The manufacturing process conforms to the environmental
regulations of the country of origin.

DAN WALKER

DESERT THIEVES

OXFORD

UNIVERSITY PRESS

1

Rain battered the streets, collecting in big, black puddles that splashed up onto the skirts and trousers of passers-by. A man towing a cart of flowers sidestepped a particularly wide pool, then hopped down off the pavement and onto the road. Dodsley Brown watched him from the shadows on the other side of the street. In his hand he held a coin which he flipped every now and then, its metal edge glinting orange in the street light. He glanced up at the clock above the baker's. Twenty-five past nine. Time to go in.

Across the street, a woman paused to open her umbrella. Dodsley waited for her to pass, then flicked the collar of his overcoat and stepped into the light. Hunching to avoid the worst of the rain, he jogged across the street, each footstep throwing up a fresh shower. He was heading towards a squat building, tucked between two taller establishments. To its front were a handful of tables and chairs, and tacked in weathered letters above the doorway were the words 'Mika's Tavern'. A man guarded the entrance.

Security.

He was a burly fellow, with a few too many muscles and scars to be likeable on first sight. He stood with his hands folded across his chest, grimacing at the rain and seeming furious enough about it to whack the next person who crossed his path.

'What do you want?' he snarled at Dodsley.

'Hello,' said Dodsley, affecting a charming voice. 'Do I know you? I don't think I've seen you before.'

The guard eyed him. 'You'd need to be a lot tougher to know me.'

'No doubt. Well, if you'll excuse me . . .' Dodsley pushed past the man.

The guard moved to block his path. 'You? In here? I don't think so.'

Dodsley halted. He glanced up at the man, who had to be a full foot taller and wider than him. He figured he'd have as much chance in a fight as a prawn against a great white shark. Dodsley stepped back. 'You know,' he said, 'I bet guarding at Mika's doesn't pay as much as you'd like.'

The guard shrugged. 'I ain't a millionaire.'

'I wonder,' Dodsley reached into his overcoat, 'if I was to provide some compensation,' he pulled out a coin and flashed it before the guard's eyes, '. . . whether you might be prepared to let me through?'

The guard glanced at the coin. 'Mika told me to be on the lookout for bribes. "Bribes come from the Aviation Army," he said.' He leaned into Dodsley to get a closer look. 'You wouldn't be Aviation Army, would you?'

Dodsley clenched his teeth. This knucklehead wasn't part of the plan. He had a deal. The usual guard would let him through no questions asked, and on his way out Dodsley would bring a mug of beer. But this new guard didn't seem the type to bend the rules for a mug of beer.

Dodsley glanced again at the clock. Nine twenty-seven. 'Listen,' he said, brightening his tone, 'what would it take for you to let me in?'

'What it takes for everyone. The password.'

Dodsley frowned. He'd known the password at one time, back when Mika had first set up the tavern and Dalmacia was a much quieter city. Was it something to do with fish? Or coffee? That's right, coffee! Or was it beer? He sighed. It was no use.

'Password?' he said, feigning ignorance. 'There's a password?' He stepped back and glanced up at the sign. 'Where am I again?'

'Mika's,' said the guard. 'And if you want to stay here instead of going to hospital, you're going to get out of my face.'

'Mika's?' said Dodsley. 'I thought this was Yarnham's! Apologies. I've been leading you on a right merry chase. It's Yarnham's I'm after. You couldn't remind me where that is, could you?'

The guard looked at Dodsley suspiciously, then nodded down the street. 'That way and take a left.'

'Much obliged,' said Dodsley. 'I'll be seeing you.'

He started to walk down the pavement in the direction the guard had indicated, feeling the guard's eyes burrow into his back, then rounded a corner and merged into the shadows.

'Damned bouncers,' he muttered. He'd come to a stop near an alley at the rear of the tavern. Tearing off his coat, he searched grumpily for somewhere to hide it. The only spot even remotely dry was a metal dustbin wedged up against the wall. Dodsley folded the coat, lifted the lid and dumped it inside. 'Nothing ever runs smoothly.'

Dodsley turned up his shirtsleeves and glanced at the stone wall separating Mika's from the alley. Even in the darkness he could make out a line of glass and rocks running along the top. He stared down at his hands wistfully, sighed once, then sprinted at the wall as fast as he could. Leaping feet-first, he hooked his toes into a gap between two rocks and propelled himself up. Near the top, he gripped the wall and snaked his torso over, before swinging his legs around and dropping down. After landing safely, he smiled, brushed himself off, and headed inside.

2

For a professional thief like Dodsley, Mika's tavern was the only tavern—dark, dingy, and ugly. A hub of illicit deals, it formed the centre of a criminal web of shadowy characters who either wanted something stolen or were looking for something to steal. All deals took place out in the open. Mika's harboured no secrets—especially from the barman himself, who provided the liquor and did his best to pay off the Aviation Army when they came snooping.

Even discounting the tavern's reputation for providing good, honest criminal work, Dodsley liked Mika's. It was a cavern, full of booths, nooks, crannies, and barely enough light to read. He liked the clientele, too. They were the sky thieves of the ground. No, better than sky thieves. They were city thieves, and a city thief's life was nothing short of thrilling. Certainly better than eking out an existence down at the docks, or in one of the city's smoke-spewing factories.

Dodsley slipped into the tavern, scanned the room for undercover Aviation Army soldiers, then selected an empty booth in the corner. He glanced at the clock above the bar.

Nine twenty-nine.

He knew little of the man he was about to meet. Their deal involved an expensive artefact which Dodsley would steal from a museum on the edge of town. It was an expensive item, which is what had piqued Dodsley's interest. But Dodsley had learned from experience that anyone requesting such an item deserved a little investigation. He hadn't got far. Indeed, when he'd tried to find out more, he'd come up against a well-constructed wall of smoke and mirrors. This had only made the job seem more interesting. Dangerous, but interesting.

From out of his trouser pocket, Dodsley pulled a burgundy flat cap and placed it on his head. The instruction to wear the hat had accompanied the note containing the location of their meeting—a way to help his employer recognize him, Dodsley figured. As he smoothed the cap onto his head, a barmaid approached and asked if he wanted a drink. Dodsley ordered some water, then shooed her away. With one eye fixed on the door, he watched the clock tick over to half-past, then the second hand as it worked its way around to thirty.

'Mr Brown?'

Standing to Dodsley's left was a big man, wider even than the guard. In the shadows behind the first was another, dressed all in black, his back turned and a top hat perched on his head. Dodsley leaned around to get a better look, but the big man moved to block his view.

'Are you Mr Brown?' asked the big man again, impatient.

'Y-Yes,' said Dodsley. 'Dodsley Brown.'

'I hope you're not this nervous when you're stealing my artefact, Mr Brown,' said the second man, remaining hidden. His voice was calm. 'I've heard good things about you. I wouldn't want you to let me down.'

Dodsley wasn't sure where to aim his words, so he spoke to the big man. 'I won't,' he said. 'I won't.'

'And you know where the object is?' said the second man. 'You've been given the location?'

'Yes,' said Dodsley.

'Good. There's a quiet country road just outside the gate that leads to the west of the city. If all's well, take the artefact there tomorrow at six. An associate of mine will wait by a willow tree next to the river. I shall have him wear a cap similar to the one you're wearing. You will receive half of your payment from him, and the other half from me once I'm satisfied with the goods. Any questions?'

Dodsley grimaced. 'Without being rude,' he said, 'I generally like to know who I'm doing business with. What's your name?'

The man in the shadows chuckled. 'My name is something you have no need of, Mr Brown. You're only here to receive orders. If that isn't satisfactory . . .'

7

Dodsley cut him off. 'No, no, no, it is, it is! I just like to do business on personal terms, that's all.'

The big man bristled at Dodsley's continued rudeness and bunched his hands into fists. Behind him, the second man fell silent, as if he was considering what to say. Dodsley felt the temperature in the room rise, and he noticed for the first time that the tavern had gone quiet.

'You can call me the Man in Black,' said the voice, eventually.

'OK.'

'I think that concludes our business, Mr Brown. Do you agree?'

'Yes.'

To Dodsley's left, the barmaid arrived with his drink. Distracted, Dodsley nodded for her to place it on the table. He reached for the glass and took a sip—the iced water cool in his mouth. When he'd finished, he placed it back down on the table to get it out of his shaking hand, then turned back to the two men. But they had gone.

Dodsley slumped back in the booth. A weight floated off his shoulders. There was something scary about the Man in Black. He didn't seem to care about the danger of capture or jail, as if robbery were as easy as walking down the road. It made Dodsley shudder to think what else might be easy for such a man . . . 'You're involving yourself with some serious people there,' said a voice over Dodsley's shoulder. Mika, the barman, was leaning on the edge of his booth, a cloth slung over his shoulder and an apron clinging to his belly.

'Nothing I can't handle, Mika.'

'These are dangerous times, son. Did you ever hear of the Dirtpath Robberies?'

Who hadn't? The Dirtpath Robberies had dominated the newspapers for the last year—a series of hold-ups along an isolated stretch of road that linked Dalmacia to nearby market-town Ryneston. In itself, cart-robbery wasn't unusual. But most highwaymen plundered carts and set their owners free. The Dirtpath robbers, on the other hand, took the booty and—without fail—murdered its owners. So far, there had been sixty deaths and not a single arrest. Farmers in the surrounding villages were terrified, locking their doors and not venturing on the roads at night.

'Of course,' said Dodsley. He took another sip of water.

Mika nodded towards where the second man had been standing. 'They reckon that's the guy.'

'Him?'

'So they say. Only someone as cold as that could pull off the Dirtpath Robberies. The Aviation Army lads are starting to put a name to him, too . . .'

Dodsley looked at Mika directly for the first time.

'But I expect a strapping lad like you knows what he's doing,' said Mika, throwing up his hands. 'You don't need an old busybody like me telling you how to run your own business. Speaking of which,' he said, his tone brightening, 'it's time I got back to mine.'

Mika padded back to the bar and started to draw a mug of ale for his next customer. In his booth, Dodsley realized his hand was shaking and slammed the glass onto the table. A sliver chipped away and spun off down the wood. Dodsley stared at it, thinking about what Mika had said, and a rage started to build inside. He pushed himself out of the booth and stamped off towards the door, unconcerned whether he'd run into the guard. As he ducked under the arch, he stopped and turned to Mika. 'Mika, that guy, the one with the robberies?'

Mika stopped shining the glass in his hand and placed it on the bar. 'What about him?'

'You said he had a name.'

'I did.'

Dodsley stared at Mika, waiting for him to speak. Mika returned his stare, then rolled his eyes. 'There's only one guy the Aviation Army thinks is nasty enough to do the Dirtpath Robberies,' he said, lowering his voice.

'Yes?'

Mika took a breath. 'Lendon Kane.'

3

'Just a couple more inches,' said Bucker, leaning over Zoya's shoulder. 'Three at the max and you're on target.'

'I can see that, you dipstick. Just focus on holding it steady.'

The sun was shining down on the deck of the *Dragonfly*, casting a faint orange glow. Like most Dalmacian summer days, this was a beautiful one, with a cool breeze and a cloudless, blue sky. The ship cut through the air like a bird, making barely a noise as it drifted alongside the Dalmacian mountain range on its way out to sea. On deck, the crew scuttled about, ferrying food and drink, and tables and chairs. Directing them was Bucker's mother, Rosie—pointing left or right depending on the load. So stunning was the weather, even the Doc was up on deck, away from his cavernous lab, leaning against the gunwale with a pair of binoculars around his neck and a smile on his face. Behind him, commanding the bridge at the stern of the ship, was pilot Cid Lightfoot. From his pipe he drew a lungful of smoke and exhaled.

Above the deck, perched high among the masts and solar sails, were Zoya DeLarose and Bucker Blake. The former, crouched, her eyes fixed above the rim of an empty bean can, shoved away the latter, who was leaning over her shoulder to get a look. Trailing away from the can were two lengths of stretched rubber, the end of each attached to a separate mast. Resting on the edge of the lookout pod was a bowl of strawberries.

'It's steady,' said Bucker. 'I'm the best knot-tier on this boat. If either of those bands comes free, you can fire one of these at me.'

Zoya pulled her head away from the can and arched an eyebrow. 'Don't tempt me Bucker. Do not tempt me.' She returned to the can and tugged backwards on it slightly, stretching the bands. Without moving her head, she gestured to the pot, 'strawberry, please.'

Bucker leaned over, selected the juiciest berry on offer and placed it into Zoya's outstretched hand. Once Zoya felt it, she brought it around to her front and dropped it into the can. It made a satisfying thud. 'Now, are you sure you want me to hit Cid?' she said. 'It is his birthday. You know how grumpy he gets.'

'That's exactly why I want to go for him,' said Bucker.

Zoya shrugged, then positioned the can so that it was aimed directly at Cid's head. She pulled back until the two rubber bands were taut, counted down from three, then let go. The strawberry arced through the air—a long, looping shot that lined up perfectly with Cid's wrinkled forehead. The kids watched it start to plummet, gaining speed every second until it splatted directly onto its target. For a moment, the world stopped as the squashed red flesh dripped down Cid's goggles and onto his T-shirt. Then one of the pilot's deputies spotted what had happened and started to laugh. It was only a small chuckle, but it spread and spread until all of the pilot crew were pointing and laughing.

Cid didn't react at first. Instead, he extracted a handkerchief from his back pocket and started to wipe away the mess. When he was finished, he folded the handkerchief, laid it down on the edge of the bridge and called to one of his deputies. 'Scott?'

'Yes sir?'

'Could you nip to the cupboard and fetch my slingshot please?'

'Yes sir. And the eggs?'

'Oh yes,' said Cid, glancing up at Zoya and Bucker, 'we'll definitely be needing those.' Cid smiled the smile of a man about to get revenge. 'Oh children,' he called. 'Oh children . . .'

Zoya leaned over the edge of the pod. 'Yes?'

'Ah, Zoya,' said Cid. 'And would Bucker be with you, by any chance?'

Bucker poked out his head.

'Ah, there he is. Now, can either of you remind me what I said I was going to do if you threw anything at me on my birthday?'

'Make us a cake?' said Bucker.

'No,' said Cid, 'it wasn't a cake. It did involve eggs, though.'

Zoya leaned into Bucker. 'We'd better get out of here.'

Bucker nodded and started to rise. As he did, Scott returned to Cid with the slingshot and a bowl of eggs. Without giving the kids a chance to run, Cid selected the biggest, loaded it into his slingshot and sent it crashing into the mast above their heads. The yellow mush splattered off the pole and dripped into Bucker's hair, causing him to claw at it with his hands. Zoya burst into laughter, until a moment later Cid's second shot crashed directly into her shirt. 'Are you kidding me?' she said. 'I just cleaned this!'

'I've got . . .' Cid paused to count, '. . . seven eggs left in this bowl. I suggest you two start running.'

Bucker's eyes flashed. He started to make his way back to the can to fire another strawberry, but Zoya grabbed his shirt and shook her head. She had to hand it to Cid—the three of them had been trading practical jokes all week, but the pilot always seemed a step ahead. If there was one thing Zoya had learned, it was that once you gained Cid's attention, the best thing you could do was run.

So she ran. She catapulted herself over the edge of the crow's nest and started to shimmy along the mast and down the netting. As she descended, she fought to keep as much of the airship as possible between her and Cid's slingshot. But it was no use. Every few seconds she felt another egg thump into her back and a gooey mess trickle down her trousers. She reached the deck and doubled over, gasping for breath. Glancing behind, she tried to work out where Bucker had got to, but he was nowhere to be seen. It was then Zoya realized her mistake: when it came to jokes, never trust Bucker Blake.

She swung her head back up to the lookout, where she spied the open mouth of a can, inside of which was another strawberry. Bucker let this go, sending the fruit shooting through the air and squishing into Zoya's face. Directly above, Bucker grinned.

'You see,' said Cid, approaching her with a towel, 'you've got to get up mighty early to trick the crew of the *Dragonfly*.' And with that, he re-lit his pipe and went off chuckling down the deck.

4

Captain Vaspine emerged from his quarters a moment later. He strode down the deck sporting a broad smile, high-fiving those within reach and waving at anyone further off. He halted when he spotted Zoya's food-splattered clothes and stared at her with a puzzled look, then shook his head and continued. As he approached the mainmast, he clicked his fingers at a few crew members and pointed to where he was heading, so that when he arrived he was accompanied by a train of thieves. Amongst these were Rosie and—because she never liked to miss any gossip—Zoya.

'See Rosie, I told you we'd have a nice day,' said the captain.

Rosie nodded. 'You also said that yesterday, and it rained all day!'

'Well, I can't always be right.' The captain winked at Zoya. 'Just most of the time. How are preparations going?'

'Good,' said Rosie. 'Really good. I've got a couple of men grabbing tables from the mess hall as we speak, and

Charlie's prepared most of the food. God knows how, he's even managed to locate fifty candles for the cake. Not sure how Cid'll feel when he sees them, mind.'

The captain glanced over at the pilot, who was back on the bridge now, staring at the scenery, idly steering the ship with one hand and patting the ash out of his pipe with the other. 'You don't mind that you're getting old, do you Cid?' shouted the captain. 'What's it you always say, "with age comes experience"?'

'You'll all experience the back of my hand in a minute if you don't shut up!' yelled the pilot.

Vaspine chuckled, then returned his attention to the pirates around him. 'And you boys,' he said, addressing the three thieves to his left, 'are you all set with the music?'

'We've got twenty songs ready. After that we can take requests.'

The captain smiled. 'Excellent.' He turned back to Rosie. 'I see you've got everything under control.'

'Of course.'

'Just checking,' said Vaspine. 'Can't let the old man's fiftieth pass without a fanfare, can we?'

The captain raised his voice again when he said the word 'fiftieth', causing Cid to shake his head. 'Just wait until you're fifty, Carlos.'

'Long time yet . . .' said Vaspine, '. . . for a twenty-one-year-old like me.'

Cid rolled his eyes.

'Good job,' said Vaspine, speaking again to the party organizers, 'That man's done more for this ship than anyone. He deserves a good night, and we're going to give it to him. Get back to it.'

At the captain's command, the sky thieves hustled back to work—Rosie to supervise the seating, and the musicians to tune their instruments. Without a job of her own, Zoya started to wander back to her cabin to change her clothes. She'd moved less than a few feet before Vaspine called her back. 'One second, Zoya, I wanted to run something by you. Where's Buck?'

Zoya looked up, prompting the captain to follow. Bucker was balanced on a crossbeam above their heads, his legs dangling and his hands clasped behind his head.

'Get down,' said Vaspine.

Bucker dropped to the deck.

'Right, you two both know you mean the world to Cid, don't you?'

Zoya and Bucker looked at their feet. 'I guess.'

'I was thinking,' said the captain, 'when we're handing out presents this evening it would be nice if you two gave him yours first. I think that would mean a lot.'

Bucker smiled. 'Yeah, nice idea.'

'I thought you'd like it. Zoya?'

Zoya nodded enthusiastically. 'Oh, definitely. Yes.'

18

Vaspine clapped his hands. 'Excellent. Now, Zoya, I think you'd better clean up, before the gulls start pecking.'

With that, he started back to his quarters. When he was gone, Bucker made his way over to the gunwale and pulled himself up. Zoya followed.

'That's cool isn't it?' he said. 'First up with the presents.'

'Yes,' said Zoya, kicking the deck.

'Talk about getting in his good books, he's going to love us after this.'

'Yes,' said Zoya.

'So what present did you get him?' asked Bucker.

'You tell me yours first.'

'You know mine,' said Bucker. 'I made him that pipe-holder.'

'Oh yes.'

'So?'

Zoya grimaced. 'I forgot.'

'What?'

'I forgot.'

'You forgot?' said Bucker.

Zoya nodded.

'How? His party's all anyone's been talking about for weeks!'

'I know,' said Zoya. 'Oh, I don't know, I guess I just . . . forgot. What am I going to do?'

Bucker jumped down. 'You're going to have to come up with something.'

Before Zoya could ask if he had any ideas, Rosie called to Bucker from the other side of the deck. 'Bucker, come and help me with these!' She shook a handful of cutlery.

'OK,' said Bucker, slumping his shoulders. 'Sorry Zo, I've got to go. I'll have a think. If I see you in time, I'll tell you. Make sure you come up with something, though. You don't want to stand up in front of everyone without anything!'

Bucker jogged off, leaving Zoya alone on the port side. 'I know,' she muttered. Then she started to walk back to her cabin, racking her brain to try to think of a plan.

5

Zoya scrubbed her clothes in a bucket of soapy water and hung them to dry on a makeshift line strung across her room. As she worked, she tried desperately to think of something she could make for Cid's birthday. Bucker's idea of a pipe-holder was great, but she couldn't steal it. And it was also too late to buy him any rare tobacco. He always looked after his clothes, so there was no point trying to make him anything new. He didn't read, he didn't draw, he didn't play cards, nothing.

Zoya stamped her feet. 'Dammit.' How had she forgotten to get him a present? She'd known his birthday was coming; Vaspine had been teasing him about it for weeks. And Rosie had reminded her and Bucker to get him a gift a week ago. At the time, Zoya had toyed with the idea of taking the bungee gear out one night and painting a mural on the side of the airship, something he could see every time they passed a still lake or pulled into one of the chrome air-docks.

She collapsed onto her bed and grabbed a coin from her bedside table. Flicking it into the air, she caught it as it dropped and flung it again, each time higher than the last. Zoya had pilfered the coin a week before from an aviation museum just outside Dalmacia. Having taken a liking to the object on the way in, she'd resolved to steal it before leaving. She'd managed it easily, distracting the guard by running down the corridor yelling something about a smoking airship in the sky, then doubling back and smashing the case while everyone was busy trying to get a look.

It was to the museum that Zoya's mind tumbled as she tried desperately to think of a present for Cid. During the same visit, the pilot had taken a shine to a pair of goggles that—according to the display case—had once belonged to the legendary sky thief, Fixyx. Whether the goggles really had belonged to the female captain, Zoya was dubious. But such issues had hardly concerned Cid. The mere chance that Fixyx had once owned the goggles left him hanging off the display case for an hour.

A plan started to form in Zoya's mind. The *Dragonfly* was currently passing Dalmacia on its way out to sea. If she could get down to the city, steal the goggles and return to the airship in time for the party, no-one need ever know she'd forgotten.

She popped the coin in her pocket, jumped off her bed and raced outside to the nearest gunwale. Climbing up, she surveyed the view. Off to the left, a dozen miles away, stood the Dalmacian mountains—grey-purple giants tinged white at the top by a covering of snow. Ahead, stretched a vast, blue ocean, twinkling in the sun. To their right and a little behind, glowed a desert jewel: Dalmacia, one of the grandest and most majestic cities on the planet. It wasn't the first time Zoya had seen Dalmacia from the sky, but it left her breathless all the same. The great wall, as solid as ever, ringed the city like a second range of mountains, intractable and unmoveable. Sprouting out of this was such a jungle of buildings that it was difficult to tell where one district ended and another began. Zoya estimated the city to be five miles away. The museum was around the other side, meaning to get there she'd have to fly around the wall (no airships were allowed to fly above the city unless they were Aviation Army or had sought express permission from the mayor) and through a wasps' nest of sky-thief airships.

It wasn't the most sensible idea Zoya had ever conceived. And yet, wasn't she a sky thief? Wasn't stealing what sky thieves did? Surely it was her duty! And if she was really honest with herself, she hadn't done anywhere near enough of it in the year since Kane's attack.

Yes, Zoya decided, she'd go down to Dalmacia and rob the goggles. She just needed to work out how.

6

There were two ways down to the surface from a moving airship. The first was to strap on a parachute and hope nobody had stolen the cord. The second was to take a transporter. Up until a couple of months previously, Zoya would have chosen the first option as she had no idea how to start up a transporter, let alone fly one. However, during the past two months, upon a request from the captain, Cid had spent a few hours each week with Zoya teaching her how to fly, in the hope she'd one day act as getaway pilot during airship raids. Zoya had been reasonably quick to pick up the skill, although she still struggled with taking off and landing. A number of holes remained in the *Dragonfly*'s hull to prove this. Still, she felt confident that if she could get hold of a transporter, she could get down to the museum and back in one piece. That was good enough for Zoya.

Securing a transporter was another matter. After the incident with Kane and the *Shadow*, the *Dragonfly* had sacrificed one of its crafts to hand in Kane's men. This had left the ship with one working transporter. For this reason, Captain Vaspine had taken to hanging the key in his quarters, with the warning that if anyone wanted to use it they had to get his permission. Zoya already knew what the captain's answer would be if she asked for this now, and she wanted to keep from him that she'd forgotten Cid's present. But Zoya needed that transporter. And that meant she had some more stealing to do.

The thought of going behind Vaspine's back made Zoya gulp, but she started off in the direction of his quarters all the same. When she arrived, she knocked heavily on the door.

'What is it?' came a voice from inside.

'It's Zoya. Can I come in?'

'Of course, you don't have to ask.'

Zoya pushed open the door and stepped inside. The captain's cabin was as jumbled as ever, with books, clothes, weapons, dinner plates, mugs, and glasses strewn all over the floor. The captain was hunched over the skymap, repositioning a model of the *Dragonfly*.

'What do you reckon to here?' he asked, nodding down at the model.

'For what?' asked Zoya.

'The party,' said Vaspine. 'I reckon it'll give us a nice view of the city on the right and the mountains on the left.'

25

Zoya pretended to look at the map. 'Looks good,' she said. 'How long until we arrive?'

Vaspine scrunched up his face. 'Another few hours—four, five.'

Zoya smiled inwardly.

'What's up?' asked Vaspine, returning his attention to the model.

'Oh it's Rosie,' said Zoya. 'She said she was having some trouble fitting all the tables and chairs on deck. She asked me to come and get you.'

Vaspine stared at Zoya. 'She wants my help with chairs?'

Zoya nodded.

Vaspine sighed. 'I don't know how these people put on their underpants in the morning. I really don't. Where is she?'

'On centre deck,' said Zoya.

Vaspine stomped out of the door, chuntering under his breath about getting a new crew and something about a long holiday. Zoya stood in silence. She hadn't expected it to be so easy. Tiptoeing to where the transporter key was hanging on the wall, she hesitated briefly as she reached out to unhook it, her hand dangling an inch from the key.

Stealing from Vaspine made her hairs stand on end, but Zoya knew it was for a good cause. If her plan was to work, she had no time for second thoughts. 'Second thoughts get you caught' was what Vaspine always told her. With the key in her pocket, she crept to the window, glanced outside, then opened the door and headed out.

To be on the safe side, Zoya avoided the transporter bay's main entrance and headed instead towards a secret one Bucker had shown her last time they'd sneaked out for a midnight bungee jump. This secret entrance was actually a narrow gap between two cabins near the captain's quarters. Zoya headed there now. Running along the left cabin was a wooden partition. She scurried up this, then crawled along Vaspine's roof, across an overhang and finally onto the mess hall. She dropped to her belly and slithered along to the corner. 'Let's see who's there then,' she muttered.

The transporter bay was a small, triangular space to the ship's bow. Scattered over the deck were dozens of sacks and crates, piled so high that Zoya and Bucker often used them to play hide and seek. Strapped to the gunwale, beside a hinged opening, was the transporter: a metal oblong slightly smaller than Zoya's cabin. It had no roof, allowing the crew quick access when escaping a robbery. Zoya adored this. There was nothing nicer on a sunny day than to head out in the transporter and whizz through the sky, the wind in her hair.

Zoya scanned the loading bay. She saw only one person, a woman unloading supplies for Cid's party. Zoya watched her, drumming her fingers quietly on the roof. Eventually, the woman packed up and ambled away down the alley. When

Zoya was sure she'd gone, she swung her legs over the edge of the roof and dropped to the deck. She tiptoed to the alley to check no-one else was coming, then darted back to the transporter. Working quickly, she removed the straps from the vehicle and tied them to the hull. She was just about to jump inside when she froze.

How was she going to start the engine without anyone hearing?

In her rush, Zoya had neglected this crucial part of the plan. And if someone did hear, it would rapidly get back to Vaspine or Rosie or Cid. Not only would her plan be ruined, she'd also be in big trouble. *No*, thought Zoya, *there's only one thing for it*. It wasn't a plan about which she was entirely happy, but it would have to do. She ran to the back of the transporter, kissed her locket for luck, and braced herself to push. 'Zoya, you're a stupid girl,' she muttered. 'A stupid, stupid girl.'

7

Zoya shoved the transporter across the deck. It moved slowly at first, then quicker, until it was sliding with ease towards the hinged opening in the side of the ship. The vehicle's front poked out over the edge and began to tip, forcing its rear into the air and Zoya with it. A second later, the transporter had tipped fully and was starting to fall under its own weight. Zoya dived forwards and pulled herself inside, grabbing a safety bar as the craft started to plummet. Above, the *Dragonfly* receded at an alarming speed. A panic swelled inside her. Suddenly, trying to start a transporter mid-air didn't seem like such a good idea. Zoya had tried a similar trick previously with Cid during one of their lessons, ('transporters ain't perfect, kid. Everyone's going to have to mid-air at some point. You might as well learn while I'm here!') which meant she knew she had about ten seconds to get the vehicle started before the increased pressure would prevent the engine catching.

But starting the engine would be difficult. The vehicle was falling front-first and the only way Zoya could stay with it was by clinging to the safety-bar, her legs kicking in the air above. With one hand still clamped to the rail, she let go with her other and felt for the key in her pocket. She wrenched it out against the buffeting wind, then dragged herself along the rail towards the pilot's seat. She counted in her head as she moved—'ten, nine, eight . . .' She made it to the ignition by five, and had strapped herself in by four. She pushed the key in the ignition and turned.

Nothing.

Zoya replaced the key and tried again. This time, the engine whirred momentarily, buzzed a little, then died.

Two seconds.

The transporter was tumbling so fast now that Zoya could barely hear. She pulled the key out, thrust it in again and turned. Once more the engine revved to life, but this time it juddered violently before starting to tick over. The engine rumbled, before coughing and spluttering. Then, as if the craft had been hit by a boulder, the air-brakes kicked in, the fans buzzed on, and the transporter slowly righted itself.

Zoya slumped into the pilot's seat and released her breath. The air was still, now. She made a couple of visual checks to ensure the transporter's instruments were working, then glanced up to see if she could still see the *Dragonfly*. She spotted it, a speck against the glow of the sun. If anybody had seen her leave, the ship would start to descend and her plan would be over. But there was little she could do to change that, so she turned back to the job at hand.

Her wristwatch read just after two. That meant she had four hours to get down to the museum, steal the goggles, escape safely, and return to the *Dragonfly* without anyone noticing. 'You don't make things easy on yourself, do you?' she muttered.

Zoya leaned into the navigation panel. Down its middle ran a thick crack that fanned at the edges. Peering past this, she studied the map, which seemed to suggest she was somewhere over the other side of the world. Zoya sighed, then loosened her belt and stood so she could see over the edge of the transporter. The vehicle had settled with its bow facing land and its stern facing the ocean. To Zoya's right, mountains soared out of the ground and ahead the city twinkled in the sun. Gripping the steering stick, she nudged the transporter so it was aimed at the city's leading edge, then gunned the engine. The transporter increased in speed, until the city started to grow, its wall soaring above her. Air traffic swarmed around the city. In her immediate airspace alone she could spy a couple of cruisers, a handful of transporters, an Aviation Army patrol ship, five airbuses and at least two sky thief ships. Zoya was untroubled by the cruisers, the airbuses, and even the Aviation Army patrol, but not the sky thieves. Small crafts like hers were a liability against pirate ships, which could manoeuvre into position behind her, open their hulls and swallow her whole. And if that happened, Zoya could kiss goodbye to the world.

Blocking her route now were two inverted, L-shaped columns, erected by the city's engineers to keep the aging wall from crumbling under its own weight. Hugging the barrier was the Aviation Army patrol ship, while to Zoya's right hovered one of the sky thief airships. This craft was significantly bigger than the *Dragonfly*, and teemed with lookouts, reminding Zoya of a spider on a web, ready to pounce. Slow though it might be, Zoya didn't fancy a sky chase any more than she fancied landing on the deck of the Aviation Army airship and introducing herself.

Zoya sat motionless in the transporter, racking her brain to think of a way past. Then it hit her. From the sky thieves' position, the Aviation Army patrol ship had to be hidden. One of the L-shaped support columns was leaning at just the correct angle to obscure their view. If Zoya could coax the sky thieves into chasing her, they'd unwittingly expose themselves to the Aviation Army. In the ensuing chaos, Zoya could sneak away.

The plan sounded good in Zoya's head, but then most plans sounded good in her head. Still, it was better than returning to the *Dragonfly* empty-handed, ready for the biggest telling-off of her life. Zoya shook her head. It would take more than a sky chase to scare her. She took one last glance at the Aviation Army ship, one deep breath, then closed her eyes and gunned the engine.

The motor roared beneath her—a deep, heavy growl that cut through the air in all directions. It took the lookouts on the sky thief ship a short while to locate her, but when they saw Zoya so close to their hull they whirled into action, strapping their weapons to their backs and climbing into lookout pods. Even the captain—a bulky, tanned, leather-faced man wearing a black bandana—peered at her through a pair of binoculars. It was whilst watching the captain that Zoya first heard the fizzing noise on the starboard side of her transporter. She heard it again a moment later, this time followed by a series of flashes on the wall nearby, then more fizzing and a *thunk* by her feet as something lodged in the transporter's hull. Zoya glanced at the sky thief airships, where a ribbon of gun barrels now lined the gunwale.

They weren't chasing her. They were trying to shoot her down.

Zoya dived down in her seat and tried to fight a sickening panic, but her thoughts were pierced by yet another bullet. This one clattered into the transporter's port side, sending a metallic ringing through her ears.

Zoya powered the engine and felt the acceleration drive her body into the pilot's seat. The transporter lurched forwards, so that Zoya had to poke her head above the side of the craft to see where it was going. Transporters were built to withstand a good deal of damage—and Vaspine had modified the *Dragonfly*'s to take more than most—but an entire ship's arsenal was not something theirs had encountered before and Zoya didn't fancy its chances. She glanced over the edge of the vehicle and saw it was heading straight for the sky thieves. She nudged the steering stick to the left, so the transporter swung slightly away. Zoya spotted the pirates on deck, wheeling a cannon into position. They loaded into it an iron ball about the size of her head, then swung the cannon so it was aimed ahead of her ship. Zoya's hands started to shake. She let out a small, terrified squeak, then closed her eyes.

One second.

Two.

Zoya opened her eyes. Instead of a cannonball, she saw a hole in the sky thief airship where the cannon had been. The hole was ringed by fire, and the men nearby were scattering in all directions. To its left, another chasm opened, this too ringed by fire. For a moment, Zoya couldn't work out what was happening. Then suddenly, she understood. Unclipping her seatbelt, she pulled herself upright, unafraid. Rearing up ahead of her, like a horse ready to charge into battle, was the Aviation Army patrol ship.

Zoya pumped her fist, then grabbed the transporter's controls. Dipping its nose, she guided the craft beneath the Aviation Army airship, fired the motor to get it back up to speed, then surged ahead. The battle continued to rage above her—a symphony of *cracks* and *whumps* and *booms* that made her flinch. She emerged out of the ship's shadow a few seconds later—the wall to her left whizzing by, each stone larger than a house. After a couple more minutes, Zoya glanced over her shoulder. The two battling vessels seemed tiny now, like toys suspended in the sky. Other airships nearby had given them a wide berth, each awaiting the arrival of Aviation Army backup. Of the two, the sky thief ship had come off worse—listing, with thick smoke billowing from its deck. Half a dozen transporters had launched from its bow and were dotted about the city wall.

Zoya blinked rapidly. If Vaspine hadn't already noticed the missing transporter, he certainly would now. She couldn't hide that much damage. Sitting in the pilot's seat, she shrugged. *Oh well*, thought Zoya, *nothing for it but to carry on now. It wouldn't do to cause all this trouble and return empty-handed*. And with that, she pulsed the engine and propelled herself into the empty sky.

8

The Dalmacian Aviation Museum was one of the most astounding, and yet least accessible, public buildings in Dalmacia. Situated a dozen miles north of the city, there was only one way to approach the museum for those too poor to own their own transporter, and that was to ride one of the cable cars that dropped from the city wall. Hundreds of visitors did this every day, forming a daisy chain of cars that glided back and forth. Zoya parked her transporter a short distance from the museum to avoid unwanted attention (how many other girls in the city could fly an airship?) then made her way straight to the arrival station and joined the throng walking up the dust path.

The museum was a mesmerizing piece of architecture. Nearly a quarter as tall as Dalmacia's surrounding wall, and of similar width, its stone bricks were sandy brown and bigger than Zoya. Scattered across its façade were lavish, golden eaves and balconies that served no real function other than to amaze. Circling the museum was an equally opulent garden, replete with ponds, trees, hedges, mazes, pathways, and water-fountains.

Zoya worked her way through the garden and up a series of shallow steps, until the path opened onto the face of the building, where a handful of ticket booths nestled into purpose-built nooks and crannies. When Cid had brought Zoya to the museum at night a month before, they'd sneaked in through a hatch in the roof after Cid had skilfully landed the transporter there. After her near miss with the sky thieves, Zoya didn't fancy her chances of getting up there without being seen. But she'd also forgotten to bring any coins.

'Hello.'

Zoya spun around to see where the voice had come from. A little girl stood by her side. 'Hello there.'

The girl had to be no older than five. She was walking alongside three other children that Zoya judged to be her brothers and sisters. Leading all four was their mother, turning every now and then to hurry them along. The little girl was pretty. She reminded Zoya of herself, with the same blond, bobbed hair and cheeky smile. She squinted up at Zoya. 'We're going to the museum.'

'Me too,' Zoya smiled.

'That's cool.'

Zoya chuckled. 'I guess it is. Have you been before?'

'No,' said the girl, scrunching up her face. 'My brother Michael says it's rubbish. I think it's going to be great.'

Before Zoya could respond, a boy walking a few feet ahead turned around. 'It's rubbish, trust me.'

'I've been before and I think it's all right,' said Zoya, aiming her comment at the girl. Michael shrugged and returned to his conversation.

'Good,' said the girl. 'Do you want to walk around with me?'

Zoya smiled. 'I would love to walk around it with you. What's your name?'

'Melissa. What's yours?'

'Zoya.'

They'd reached the back of the queue now. Zoya chatted with Melissa for a few minutes as they edged slowly forward. However, in the pleasantness of the conversation, she forgot to think of a way inside the museum. And so it was that, as Zoya reached the front of the queue and found herself amongst the other siblings, she decided to try to sneak past as one of them.

'Would you like tickets to the museum, madam?' asked the girl behind the counter.

'Yes, please,' said Melissa's mother.

The girl leaned out of the booth and made a quick count of the children, nodding at each. When it was her turn, Zoya dipped her face so it wouldn't be seen. 'So,' said the cashier, pulling herself back, 'that's . . . one adult and four children?'

The mother stared at her, puzzled, then shook her head and nodded. The girl stamped five green tickets and handed them over. 'Entrance is just over there. You have a nice day.'

Zoya shook her head in bemusement. It was amazing what you could get away with if you just had the confidence. Bucker, back on the *Dragonfly*, would have been proud.

The lobby of the museum was bustling with people— most checking their bags and coats at the baggage counter, or unfolding maps and trying to work out where to go first. Zoya wandered past the crowd towards the lobby's centre, where there was displayed a bronze statue of Jupiter, Zoya's father and one of the most famous sky thieves in the history of the world. She smiled at the statue, a sudden reminder of her heritage. In spite of a plaque requesting she refrain, Zoya rubbed her hand on the bronze, which felt smooth and cool. 'Hi Dad,' she muttered. As she did, she noticed a movement out of the corner of her eye. Beside her, Melissa was doing the same.

'It's cool isn't it?' she said.

Zoya smiled. 'Yes, he is.'

'Where are we going first then?'

Zoya glanced at the clock hanging on the far wall. Three o'clock. That meant she had three hours before she had to be back on the *Dragonfly*. Time enough to spend a little with her new friend. 'We can go wherever you want.'

'In which case,' said Melissa, spinning on her heels and peering into the multiple doorways that led off the main lobby, 'I think we should go . . . that way.'

9

She dragged Zoya off through the west wing of the museum
and proceeded to spend the next hour dragging her around
the rest too. They encountered all sorts of exhibitions,
including rooms dedicated to sky thief fashion, Aviation
Army uniforms, weapons, artwork, sculptures, replicas of
transporter engines, masts, Injektors, and much more. Indeed,
so awash was the museum with goodies, and so bursting with
enthusiasm was Melissa, that for a little while Zoya forgot
all about her mission. Only when they entered the museum's
central courtyard—famed for a treasure collection so grand
as to inspire jealousy in even the wealthiest industrialist—
did Zoya spy Cid's goggles and remember why she was there.

The goggles rested on a burgundy velvet cushion in a
glass display case in the centre of the courtyard. Two oil
lanterns were positioned either side, giving the metal a
dull shine. Seated beside the goggles was a bored-looking
guard, whose job it was to watch the item lest someone like

Zoya come along and try to steal them. Like most thieves who'd attempted to pilfer the goggles, Zoya didn't have a particularly strong interest in antique sky thieves' artefacts (in spite of her lifelong fascination with the rascals) but even she had to admit they were something special. Two oval lenses, ringed by golden airship wheels, gave way to decorative clockwork hinges that graduated into a brown, leather strap with golden studs. An information board by the goggles advised admirers that, in monetary value alone, they were worth an entire Dalmacian business district street. Sentimentally, they were worth even more.

'Have you ever seen these before?' Zoya asked Melissa, who'd crept up behind her.

Melissa glanced into the case. 'Nope.'

'These goggles,' said Zoya, lowering her voice to add drama, 'once belonged to the greatest female sky thief in history. Have you ever heard of Fixyx and her battle with Gruesome Captain Grimybeard?'

Melissa shook her head.

'Fixyx,' repeated Zoya. 'She took over the Island in the Sky? Grimybeard killed her by throwing her off the top of the Karabekian Gate?'

Melissa's eyes flashed as if she'd remembered, then she shook her head again.

'You've got a lot to learn,' said Zoya. 'When I was your age, I lived in an orphanage with lots of other children. We

41

all shared the same bedroom. And every night, just before we went to sleep, Mr Whycherley, the orphanage's owner, would read us a story. He used to read us lots of different stories, but one of our favourites was always the story of Fixyx and her battle with the gruesome captain.'

'Mum says sky thieves are bad people,' said Melissa.

'Not all of them,' said Zoya. 'Fixyx changed a lot of things. Before her there *were* no female sky thief captains. After her, there were women doctors, lawyers, everything!'

Melissa looked at the goggles with fresh eyes.

'Do you see why they're important now?'

Melissa cocked her head slightly to get a closer look at the glasses, then shrugged. 'They're OK, I guess. I want to go and look at that massive sword.'

Melissa ran off in the direction of a giant blade hanging from the wall in the corner of the courtyard. Zoya watched her slalom through the crowd until she re-joined her mother, then turned back to the goggles. Stealing them would be more difficult than she'd anticipated now she'd seen the guard. Even if she could smash the case, her chances of getting away were about as good as her chances of the guard reaching inside and giving her the goggles for free.

That meant she had to be a little more cunning. But how? She glanced around the courtyard. Perhaps there was somewhere she could hide until the evening, then jump out and snatch the goggles? But it was no use, she needed to be back for Cid's party. What about a distraction? Perhaps she could convince someone to distract the guard, while she smashed the case and ran. Too confusing. Zoya's pulse quickened in frustration. She moved away from the goggles and started to pace up and down the aisles, trying to think. After a moment, her thoughts were interrupted by a ringing sound somewhere in the distance. Zoya ignored it as best she could and continued to think. Perhaps she could convince the guard that someone was coming to steal the goggles, he would remove them and she could use the thieving skills she'd learned over the previous year to snatch them off him.

Zoya stamped her feet.

It was no good. All her ideas were stupid. 'And I wish someone would shut up that flipping ringing!'

Zoya said these last words aloud. As she did, she noticed for the first time that the courtyard was starting to empty. She could hear the ringing clearly now, a melodious *ting ting* loud enough to be heard the museum over. As Zoya searched about for its source, a neatly-dressed woman burst into the courtyard. 'Fire!' she yelled. 'Fire! Evacuate! Fire!' And with that, she disappeared into the adjoining wing, where Zoya heard her shout the same thing. Reluctantly, those still in the courtyard glanced around for confirmation the alarm was real, then started, one-by-one, to make their way to the exit.

Zoya, too, glanced about the courtyard, looking for flames or smoke. She found nothing. If there was a fire, it was somewhere else. Rapidly, she started to concoct a plan. Museum policy would dictate that everyone evacuate the building, the guards included. If she could somehow remain inside while everyone else left, she'd be able to smash the case, grab the goggles, and get away without anyone noticing.

Moving swiftly, Zoya ducked behind an ornamental bench and scudded along a low wall until she was safely concealed behind a pillar. She remained absolutely still for the next ten seconds, then leaned out her head as far as she dared. The guard was still beside the goggles, but standing now, shooing away the last of the visitors. Once he'd shepherded them safely outside, he inspected the courtyard one last time, then headed towards the exit.

Zoya emerged and tiptoed to the goggles. She glanced over her shoulder, then grabbed the guard's chair, closed her eyes and swung it at the case. A sharp *crack* rang out above even the alarm. The glass started to splinter and spit out in all directions, until the front of the case was obliterated. A ripple of excitement flowed up Zoya's spine. She reached inside to snatch the goggles, but as she did a voice from behind made her jump. 'I think you'll find those are mine.'

Lifting the goggles away, Zoya turned around slowly, expecting to see the museum guard.

Instead, she turned directly into the barrel of a gun.

10

'Not that I don't appreciate you breaking the case for me. It saved me from getting glass all over my shirt. But I didn't set fire to this place for you to snaffle the goggles from under my nose. Give them to me now and you can walk out of here, no harm done.'

Zoya took a breath. She had no intention of getting shot for a pair of goggles, golden or not. But now they were hers, and she wanted to keep them. She eyed the man to see if he was the sort to fire a gun. He was tall, a dozen or so years older than Zoya. A short sweep of hair sat above a dusky face, and a squint in his left eye made him look as if he was forever staring into the distance. But in spite of the gun, he was no sky thief. A cream, cotton grandad shirt hung over a pair of trousers and boots. Strapped to his side was an ornate gun holster that had to be worth a hundred coins. A city thief, Zoya decided. And everyone knew city thieves were small-time. They certainly lacked the guts to shoot little girls in cold blood.

She smiled.

'What?' asked the man.

'You're not going to shoot me.'

'I will if I need to.'

'You won't,' said Zoya. 'If you shoot me, not only will the Aviation Army be after you for robbery, they'll also be after you for the murder of an innocent little girl.'

'Oh yes,' said the man, arching an eyebrow, 'very innocent!'

Zoya shrugged.

The man held the gun a moment longer, then slotted it back into its holster. 'OK,' he said, 'but you're going to give me those goggles. I know a man who wants them and he's *definitely* the sort to kill a girl.'

'He wouldn't be the first person who's wanted me dead this year,' said Zoya.

The man stared at her, then lunged desperately for the goggles. Zoya anticipated his move, ducked under his arm, and started to back away towards the rear of the courtyard.

'I'm telling you kid, you don't want to cross this guy.'

'And I'm telling you, I ain't scared of anyone. So you can tell your friend if he wants his goggles he can come and get them.'

'Lendon Kane's not the kind of man you want to mess with.'

Zoya's stomach lurched to her throat. 'What did you say?'

'Yeah, I thought that would scare you.'

'No, say the name again,' said Zoya.

'Kane. Lendon Kane. The sky thief.'

Zoya shook her head. Lendon Kane was dead. Zoya had watched him fall. No-one could have survived that, not even Kane. 'Have you seen him?' she snapped.

'Kane?'

Zoya nodded.

'Not exactly,' said the thief. 'But I've spoken to him.'

Zoya scoffed. So it was an imposter. Someone pretending to be Kane to intimidate others. She felt better immediately, and returned to figuring out how she was going to escape. Keeping one eye on the thief, she scanned the courtyard to find a rear exit. Directly behind her was one of the doors the guard had closed before heading out to the front. However, to get it open Zoya was going to have to distract the thief.

'You know, I'm not a horrible girl,' said Zoya. 'I'm going to take these goggles, but I'll give you something good in return.'

The thief narrowed his eyes—interested for a split second—then shook his head. 'Nope, the goggles.'

'Over by the case,' continued Zoya, 'I've left a locket. It's worth more than the goggles.'

The thief stared suspiciously at Zoya, then glanced over his shoulder. Sensing her chance, Zoya kicked a rubbish bin into the aisle between them, then darted through the door behind her and into the north wing of the museum.

The north wing was filled with smoke—thicker at the ceiling, hazier near the floor. Zoya hacked and coughed as she breathed the smog into her lungs, frantically searching for another exit. She spotted one on the far side of the room, and started to sprint towards it, swerving left and right to avoid the display cases. She'd made it less than halfway when the thief burst through the door behind her. Zoya glanced over her shoulder, briefly caught the man's eyes, then pressed on. She reached the exit a moment later, gripped the knob and yanked hard.

Nothing.

Zoya tried the door again to make sure, but it held firm. She spun around to locate the thief, and spotted him a dozen yards away, clattering into the final display case. As soon as he realized Zoya was trapped, he regained his balance and started to walk slowly towards her. A smirk slid across his face. 'Oh dear.'

Zoya's eyes flickered rapidly, searching for another exit. To her right was a sliding window, open about five inches. Even if she'd had time to dive over before the thief reached her, opening the window would take too long. No, there had to be another way.

During her first pass through the north wing an hour or so before, Zoya had spotted a collection of ornamental swords hanging from the wall. She kicked herself up now and grabbed the nearest weapon, a bone-handled cutlass.

Swinging the sword in front of her, she used its handle to deflect the pouncing thief and send him crashing into a coin-filled display case.

The smoke was so dense now that Zoya struggled to breathe. She coughed a couple of times to clear her lungs, then took off in the direction of the window. When she arrived, she dug her fingers beneath the sliding glass and shoved it up. A gust of fresh, cool air flooded the room. Zoya sucked in a lungful as she hurled the cutlass onto the lawn outside. Glancing one last time at the thief, still writhing on the floor and rubbing his temple where he'd cracked it against the case, she patted her back pocket to make sure she still had the goggles, then pulled herself through the window.

Zoya landed on the grass with a thump. She was at the rear of the museum now—another garden, its grass fringing a small, central pond. In the distance rose the Dalmacian mountains, and a few miles to her left the towering city wall. The garden was ringed by a thick hedge, along which were posted pairs of guards. The closest of these spotted Zoya as she spotted them.

'Oi! What are you doing?'

Zoya ignored them and pushed herself up.

'Oi! I'm talking to you!'

From somewhere inside the building, Zoya heard footsteps approach the window. 'Give me a break!' she yelled. She scanned the garden quickly for an escape. Leaning against the building to her left was some scaffolding, which was being used to repair the fascia. The platform reached only a few feet above her head, but if she could scramble up and use it to jump the hedge, she might be able to get away. Zoya started to run.

'Hey!' shouted one of the guards. 'Thieves! Thieves!' He bolted inside a nearby hut and returned with a bell, which he proceeded to ring as hard as he could. 'Get them!'

Zoya glanced back. The two guards were dashing towards the thief, who'd tumbled through the window and was, in turn, sprinting towards the scaffold. Zoya reached the platform and hauled herself up to its lowest level, dropping the cutlass to prevent it weighing her down. Months of scaling the *Dragonfly*'s rigging meant she made light work of the climb, and she reached the top in seconds. Back on the ground, the thief arrived——his forehead cut where he'd banged it.

'You won't catch me,' said Zoya.

The thief hooked his hand onto the nearest rail. 'We'll see about that.'

To reach the transporter bay on the other side of the hedge, Zoya would have to leap out and away from the scaffold, then land safely. Even for a sky thief, it was quite a jump. She shook her head, then backed up to the edge of the scaffold and ran. As soon as her leading foot hit the end of the platform, she thrust her body upwards and out. A feeling of weightlessness overcame her as she soared through the air and over the hedge. As she landed, her right ankle buckled beneath her, sending her crumpling into a heap. 'Owwwww!'

The thief had reached the top of the platform now.

Zoya pushed herself up off the floor and attempted to put some weight on her injured leg, but it buckled again. A cold shiver ran down her spine. If she couldn't run, that meant she had about thirty seconds before the thief, the guards, and probably the Aviation Army caught up with her. Her only chance of escape was in one of the transporters in the landing bay.

Zoya hobbled over to the nearest transporter and swung herself inside. From somewhere behind her, she heard the thief thud into the ground, his breathing heavy and laboured. Zoya thrust him from her mind and set to work on starting the engine. Taking a hair clip from her hair, she bent it into the general shape of a key and slotted it into the ignition. She twisted it left and right, then heard the familiar *whoosh* of the engine. At exactly the same moment, a voice came over her shoulder.

'Stop!'

For the second time, Zoya turned to find herself staring into the barrel of a gun.

'Open the door,' said the thief.

Zoya stayed still, looking into the man's eyes. There was a fire in them that had been missing before. She did as she was told. The thief kept the gun trained on Zoya as he slid into the back seat. 'Where are the goggles?'

Zoya gritted her teeth. She pulled the goggles from her pocket and tossed them into his lap. 'Thank you,' said the thief. 'If you'd done this back at the museum, none of this need have happened.'

'Whatever,' said Zoya.

The thief shifted his position so he could see the hedge. The two guards were on top of the scaffold now, ready to jump. 'Listen,' said the thief, turning back to Zoya, 'I want to work with you about as much as I want a fly in my beer, but if we don't get out of here in about ten seconds, we're both going to be caught by those two fellows and there ain't going to be any escape. Can you fly this thing?'

'Maybe,' said Zoya.

'Kid!'

Zoya scowled. 'Yes. I can.'

'Do it then!' said the thief. He glanced back at the guards.

Zoya pressed the throttle. The engine buzzed, then started to push the transporter off the ground—slowly at first, then quicker. In no time at all, the museum grew small. Back on the scaffold, the guards spotted their escape and raced back to the command post to alert the Aviation Army.

'Phew,' said the thief from the back seat, 'that was close.

You know, I've never been in one of these before?' He nodded his appreciation at the transporter. 'Pretty cool.'

Zoya remained quiet.

'Listen,' said the thief, noting her silence, 'it's nothing personal. I was asked to get the goggles and that's what I'm going to do.'

'Well,' said Zoya, unimpressed, 'we've got about five minutes before the entire Aviation Army'll be after us. I hope you're ready for another chase . . .'

Before Zoya could finish her sentence, the transporter was engulfed in shadow. To their starboard side, a giant craft had manoeuvred into place like a predator stalking its prey. Zoya dropped her hand to the steering stick, ready to attempt an escape, but she held it steady. There was something familiar about the ship. She glanced up and down its hull, trying to work it out. Then the truth dawned.

Zoya wasn't looking at an Aviation Army airship.

She was looking at the *Dragonfly*.

11

Zoya grinned. 'What is it?' the thief whispered. 'Is it Aviation Army?'

'Worse,' said Zoya. 'For you, anyway. It's my ship.'

'Yours?'

Before Zoya could answer, there was a shout from above. 'Zoya, is that you?' Rosie leaned over the *Dragonfly*'s gunwale and looked down at them.

'It's me,' shouted Zoya.

Rosie turned into the ship to confer, then returned. 'Take her into the loading bay. We'll see you there.'

'No you don't,' said the thief, shaking his gun in Zoya's direction.

Zoya turned around and raised an eyebrow. 'If you pull that trigger, the entire airship will come down here and tear you to pieces. So shoot me if you like, but I wouldn't if I were you.'

The thief frowned, sighed, then lowered his weapon.

Zoya steered the transporter around the other side of the airship and lined it up with the loading bay. This new craft was slightly bigger than the *Dragonfly*'s hatch, and she had to be careful when guiding it through not to damage the hull. Once she'd safely touched down, she flicked off the engine, opened the door, and stepped gingerly down onto the deck. Lined up to meet her were Captain Vaspine, Cid, and Rosie. Rosie looked like she wanted answers, as Vaspine nodded for a group of pirates to surround the thief.

'Where've you been?' asked Rosie hugging Zoya. 'We've been so worried!'

'I went to get Cid a present.'

The pilot jerked awake at the mention of his name, then rolled his eyes and shook his head. 'Well, at least you're safe, that's the main thing,' he barked.

Vaspine hadn't spoken yet. He looked at Zoya now, irritation in his eyes. 'Who's this?' he asked, gesturing at the thief.

'I don't know,' said Zoya. She pulled away from Rosie, crossed to the transporter and took the golden goggles from the thief's lap. 'I went down to the museum to get these for Cid, and he was trying to rob them at the same time. We escaped some guards together and ... and ...' Zoya trailed off.

'What's your name?' asked Vaspine.

'Dodsley Brown,' said the thief. 'I'm Dodsley Brown.'

Vaspine glared at him, then clicked his teeth. 'You're lucky I'm in a good mood, Dodsley.' He turned to the men guarding the thief. 'Take him to the holding cell. Get him something to eat.'

The men manhandled Dodsley out of the back of the transporter and carried him off in the direction of the main deck. When they'd gone, Vaspine returned his attention to Zoya. 'And as for you, you've got a hell of a lot to answer for. I want you in my quarters in ten minutes. Dismissed.'

Zoya hobbled off towards her cabin, a sick feeling in her stomach. She'd never troubled the captain before. Now that she had, she felt the same as when Mr Whycherley had told her off at the orphanage, a little girl with her hands in the biscuit jar. Rosie caught up with her after a few steps. 'He's annoyed, you know?'

'I know,' said Zoya.

'It was pretty stupid,' said Rosie. 'What were you thinking?' She checked herself. 'On second thoughts, save that for the captain.'

Back in her room, Zoya cleaned up in a basin of water, changed her clothes, and wrapped a bandage around her ankle to give it some support. Then she trudged to the captain's quarters. The door was open when she arrived. Vaspine was sat at his desk, hunched over a piece of paper. He didn't look up when he heard her enter. 'Sit down.'

Zoya took a chair just in front of his desk. For thirty

seconds, Vaspine continued to read, before he finally lifted his head and stared at Zoya. He took a number of deep breaths, then clasped his hands together with his elbows on his desk. 'Zoya, have you ever heard of the sky thief code?'

Zoya shook her head.

'I didn't think so. It was written a hundred years or so ago, on the Island in the Sky.'

Zoya nodded to show she was listening.

'There were a bunch of rules,' continued the captain, 'just ideas to follow really, because no-one was keeping score. Some of the rules were good, some bad. Have a guess what the punishment was for breaking them.'

'Which?' asked Zoya.

'Any.'

Zoya thought. 'No idea.'

'Banishment,' said Vaspine. He let the word hang in the air. 'Any sky thief breaking one of the rules was supposed to be banished from his ship.'

Zoya looked away. She got the point. When Vaspine realized this, he removed his chin from his hands and placed them behind his head. 'You could have been killed, you know?'

'I know,' said Zoya.

'I've been doing this a long time,' said the captain. 'And so have most of the other people on this ship. You've been here a year. We're sharp enough to go off on our own. You're not, yet.'

'I know,' said Zoya.

Vaspine leaned back in his chair. 'You know?' He stared at her, then leaned forward and plucked up the paper he'd been studying when she entered. It was a single sheet, upon which were printed ten faces, each with a name and number. Zoya scanned the faces and recognized a couple, particularly those near the top. They were sky thieves.

'Do you know what that is?' asked the captain.

'I'm guessing it's a most-wanted list.'

Vaspine nodded. 'It's the Aviation Army's. Do you recognize any of them?' Zoya glanced down the list. Bang in the centre was a familiar face. 'That's not . . .'

'Dodsley Brown,' confirmed the captain. 'Number five on the Aviation Army's most-wanted list. Now do you understand why I'm so annoyed?'

Zoya looked at her feet.

'Not only did you run away from my ship, not only did you lose our transporter, not only did you force us to cancel Cid's birthday to come and rescue you, not only did you steal something ridiculous from under the city's nose, you've also returned with the Aviation Army's fifth most-wanted criminal, placing us all in danger.'

'I'm sorry,' mumbled Zoya.

'Sorry doesn't cut it. I thought you had more sense.'

Zoya shifted in her seat. 'What can I do to make it right?'

The captain rubbed the back of his neck, then got up

from his seat and walked over to the skymap. He shook his head. 'Nothing. We can't just dump the guy. And we can't kill him either. We'll just have to wait until we can set him down somewhere and hope the Aviation Army or his goddamn boss doesn't come after him in the meantime.' The captain picked up the golden goggles from off the skymap. 'What does he want with these things, anyway?'

Zoya missed the captain's question. She was thinking about what he'd said about Dodsley's boss, and in turn what Dodsley had told her. In the rush to get away from the museum, she'd forgotten all about Kane.

'Captain?'

Vaspine manoeuvred the goggles into the light of an oil lantern and peered at the metalwork. 'What?'

'When we were in the museum, Dodsley said something funny. I'm sure it's nothing, but . . .' she paused, almost unable to say the words, 'he said he was working for Lendon Kane.'

Vaspine froze, one hand wrapped around the goggles. He returned them to the table. 'Say that again.'

'He said he was working for Kane.'

The captain eyed Zoya warily, unsure whether she was joking. Zoya held his stare. 'Are you sure?'

'Yes,' said Zoya. 'I guess someone's pretending to be Kane. But still, it's a bit weird.'

'Very,' said Vaspine, rubbing his chin. 'I think it's about time we had a chat with this prisoner of ours.'

12

'Spike!' Vaspine called out of the window. A few moments later, a sky thief came running.

'Sir?'

'Fetch me the prisoner.'

Spike nodded, then scurried away. Vaspine turned back to Zoya. 'If you're lying about this to deflect my attention from your own actions, you're going to be in even bigger trouble.'

'I'm not.'

Spike returned with Dodsley, who was flanked by two crew members. Vaspine nodded for the guards to wait outside.

The crew left, leaving Vaspine, Zoya, and Dodsley alone. Zoya glanced at the thief, whose hands and feet were tied. He looked exhausted.

'Dodsley Brown, didn't you say?' said Vaspine.

The thief nodded.

'You know, Dodsley, if we handed you in to the Aviation

Army, we'd get a thousand gold coins, just like that.' The captain snapped his fingers.

'True,' said the thief. 'But thanks to your friend here, I know you're sky thieves. And no sky thief's going to fly up to an Aviation Army airbase by choice.'

Vaspine smiled. 'You're right,' he said. He turned to Zoya. 'He's right.' Zoya shrugged. 'In which case,' continued the captain, 'I'm sure you see my conundrum. On my airship, I have the Aviation Army's fifth most-wanted man. I don't want him on my airship, because then the Aviation Army's going to be after me. So what do I do?'

Catching Vaspine's meaning, Dodsley started to claw at his handcuffs. 'Whoa, whoa!'

'Do I do the nasty thing?' said Vaspine. 'Do I do what other sky thieves do in my situation? Do I cut the thief's throat and dump him off the back of the airship? Or do I leave him in the most remote part of the Island in the Sky, with no food or water?'

Dodsley's struggling became desperate. 'You can't do that!'

'But then I think to myself, no,' said Vaspine, 'you're not that kind of pirate, Carlos. Money's your game. So I think, instead, about making a deal with Dodsley Brown's boss. I hand over the punk for a few coins and we call it even.'

Dodsley stopped struggling and listened.

'But then Zoya here tells me what you said about your boss, pretending he's a dead man. And I think to myself, how am I going to make a deal with this guy's boss if he's dead?'

Vaspine eyeballed Dodsley.

'He's not dead,' exclaimed the thief. 'That's who asked me to get the goggles, I swear!'

'Kane's dead,' snapped Zoya. 'He died a year ago. I saw him!'

Vaspine silenced her with a glare. 'The girl's right,' he said, returning to Dodsley. 'He died. So, either you're working for a dead man, or you're playing with me . . .'

'No! I swear! He said his name was Lendon Kane.'

Vaspine rubbed his chin. 'This man, what did he look like?'

Dodsley shifted awkwardly. 'I've never seen him. Not face-to-face. The one time we spoke, he kept himself hidden.'

'You never saw him?'

'No,' said Dodsley. 'Just his top hat.'

Vaspine's eyes narrowed.

'It's true! It's not the kind of look you forget. Top hats aren't exactly the rage down in Dalmacia.'

Vaspine leaned back against the skymap. 'Guards!' he yelled. The guards entered. 'Take him back to his cell. I think our guest needs a little more time to think about the gravity of his situation, and when it's appropriate to make jokes.'

The guards dug their arms under Dodsley's and started

to drag him from the room. As they pulled, the thief struggled, kicking his feet against the floor. 'I swear,' he said, eyes aflame, 'I swear his name was Kane. Ask Mika in Mika's Tavern. He told me it was Kane—the guy doing the Dirtpath Robberies . . .'

Dodsley's voice became a mumble as he was dragged out of the cabin and across the deck. Vaspine and Zoya sat in silence until his voice died away, each lost in thought.

When at last the captain spoke, his tone was commanding. 'Zoya, you're not out of the woods on this one. But any punishment's going to have to wait. I want you to speak to Rosie and Cid, tell them to meet me here in fifteen minutes. Keep it secret.'

13

Zoya felt edgy as she made her way over to Rosie and Cid, so she easily spotted Bucker—a cheeky grin on his face—waiting to pounce from the mast near the captain's quarters. 'Not now, Bucker,' she said.

'Hey! You saw me.'

'It's not hard when you're right in front of me.'

Bucker flipped so that he was hanging from outstretched hands, then dropped to the deck. 'You got yourself into a bit of trouble today, didn't you?' He jogged to catch up.

Zoya ignored him.

'It's not often you get called for a roasting without me. What happened?'

Bucker jumped in front of Zoya, causing her to stop. She glared. 'I said not *now*.' She stormed past, leaving him on the deck wondering what he'd done.

Zoya found Rosie with a bunch of the crew, packing away the party gear they'd carefully laid out earlier. Rosie looked up when she saw the girl, puzzled. She quickly realized from the look on Zoya's face that the news was serious and deposited her chair on the deck. 'Now?' she said.

'In his quarters,' said Zoya, quietly.

Rosie took off her apron, then turned to the crew and ordered them to continue without her. Once she was satisfied they knew what they were doing, she nodded her thanks to Zoya and walked off towards Vaspine.

Off the ship, the sun was starting to set in a wash of pink and violet. Zoya glanced at her watch and realized it was six o'clock, the planned time of Cid's party. She surveyed the central deck, which made a sad sight in the fading light, covered in tables, chairs, plates, mugs, food, ale, wine, musical instruments, and everything else necessary for a sky thief's birthday. The sight of it produced a knot in her stomach. Even though her attempt to steal the goggles had been well-intentioned, she also knew the cancellation of the party was entirely her fault and felt terrible.

'Cheer up kid, it might never happen.'

The voice came from somewhere over her shoulder. Zoya turned around to find Cid standing near the gunwale, taking a puff at his pipe. At first, she couldn't work out why the pilot wasn't up on the bridge, flying the ship. But then she spotted something twinkling behind him, and understood. After the battle with Kane the previous year, while the *Dragonfly* was undergoing repairs, Cid had flown to Dalmacia and commissioned an engraver to make a plaque commemorating

Beebee's death. Cid was in front of the plaque now, his head bowed. 'You know, it's been a year since he died?'

'That day was your birthday?' said Zoya.

'Well, we didn't make anything of it last year, what with everything going on. But yeah, my birthday.'

'Blimey,' said Zoya.

'Don't worry about it. I never liked parties, anyway. I'd rather spend some time up here.' He ran his hand along the plaque.

Zoya smiled. 'I'm sorry Cid,' she said. 'It's all my fault. I forgot to get you a present and I wanted to get you something good. Then I remembered the goggles.'

The pilot looked up. 'And a fine present they'd have made. But I'll tell you an even finer present: knowing you're safe.'

Zoya blushed.

'It doesn't mean I'm not mad. Lord knows we've got enough to worry about with Bucker running around. The last thing we need is you joining him. But I know you won't do it again.' Cid paused to impress the point, then brightened. 'So, no hard feelings.'

Zoya nodded.

'What are you doing here anyway? Why aren't you getting some food?'

Zoya glanced down at the sun, dipping below the horizon. 'The captain asked me to fetch you. He wants you and Rosie in the cabin.'

Cid's eyes narrowed. 'Something up?'

'Maybe.' Zoya frowned. 'Best if the captain tells you.'

Cid tapped the ash from his pipe and slotted it into his pocket. 'I'd better get over there. Listen, if you're looking for a job, help the lads clear the tables.' He glanced off the ship into the distance. 'I don't know why, but I get the impression we might need a clear deck before the day's out.'

And then the pilot was gone, stepping quickly down the deck, a pensive look on his face. Zoya joined the crew and helped them get everything back into the dining hall, then stuck around and grabbed a plate of sausages and mash. She ate without speaking, allowing the conversation to flow around her. When she finished, she cleared her plate and headed to her cabin to lie down. She remained there, breathing in the cool air, until eventually she drifted off, one hand clasping her locket and the other on her sword.

The wind blew hard that evening, rattling the decks. Eerie whistles cut through howls that reminded Zoya of the creepy stories Mr Whycherley used to tell back at the orphanage. Zoya slept fitfully—tossing and turning, waking from a dark dream only to tumble into another—until she found herself truly awakened by the rhythmic flapping of a loose panel outside her cabin. She lay on her bed for a few minutes, eyes wide open, then got up, threw on some clothes and her jacket and headed outside.

It was dark on deck, the ship surrounded by a moonless sky. Even from her cabin, Zoya could hear the solar sail slapping violently against the mainmast. She unhooked an oil lantern from the wall, dimmed it so as not to make the *Dragonfly* an obvious target, then made her way towards the mast.

The wind had torn a number of objects from their strappings, and the deck was littered with sacks, barrels, buckets, and tables. Zoya had to lean into gusts to avoid being blown over, whilst simultaneously keeping an eye on deck to make sure she didn't trip. She stumbled on past the mainmast towards the bridge, where she expected to see one of Cid's deputies manning the wheel. Instead, she recognized the shadowy outline of Captain Vaspine.

'What are you doing here?' he asked.

'I couldn't sleep,' said Zoya, climbing up. She placed the lamp down on the deck, throwing shadows onto the captain's face. Vaspine looked down at the flame, then up at Zoya, and finally behind her at the violence hammering the ship.

'There's a storm coming,' he said, quietly. 'We need to be careful.'

'We'll be OK,' said Zoya. She waited before speaking again. 'Is Kane alive?'

Vaspine lifted his eyes. 'I don't know.'

'But how could he be? We saw him fall.'

The captain nodded. 'That's what I keep telling myself. But your friend's rumour isn't the only one I've heard.'

Zoya reached up to her chest and laid a hand on her locket. 'Is he coming?'

Vaspine shook his head. 'I don't know.'

Zoya slumped onto the top step. Could he be alive? If he was, it would only be a matter of time before he came. She shuddered. 'What'll we do?'

Vaspine shrugged. 'Same thing we always do. Fight.'

Even in the cold night air, Zoya felt herself burn hot. On the horizon, a faint orange light began to glow. It seemed to be some way off, although it was difficult to be sure in the dark. Vaspine turned to see what had caught Zoya's eye. Together, they watched the light grow to the size of a fist. Presently, another appeared to the right of the first, accompanied by a high-pitched squealing. It was only then that Zoya realized what was happening. The orange lights weren't fireworks, or stars, or lanterns. They were flaming projectiles, fired from a craft cloaked in darkness. And they were heading directly for the *Dragonfly*.

14

'Get down!' yelled Vaspine. He rolled the ship's wheel, then threw himself over Zoya. The projectiles hit the bridge a second later, one after the other, smashing through the deck and lodging below. Zoya and the captain opened their eyes to find they'd been flung a dozen yards down the deck in the direction of the mainmast. Ahead, the bridge had disappeared, replaced by a gaping, smoking hole. Ignoring the ringing in her ears, Zoya rolled to her feet and approached the gap. Buried twelve feet below was the cannonball, its flames licking the surrounding wood. There was another hole a few yards further towards the stern, where the other projectile had hit.

'Zoya! Move!'

Zoya flicked her head just in time to see another flaming ball plunging in on their position. She felt Vaspine's arms wrap around her waist and drag her back, sending them tumbling over each other. Zoya landed on top of the captain and watched the ball—this one slightly smaller than the last—crash through the deck and into the belly of the ship. When it was gone, she rolled off, clambered to her feet, and faced Vaspine, tears in her eyes.

'We'll be OK,' said the captain. 'Go and get Cid and Rosie. I need them here now!'

'What are you going to do?' asked Zoya.

'Just go!'

Zoya sprinted down the deck, glancing over her shoulder every few yards to make sure no more projectiles were coming. She'd made it to the mainmast when she spotted Cid, Rosie, and half the rest of the crew walking quickly towards her.

'What's going on?' asked Cid. 'Another of the Doc's experiments?'

'We're under attack,' Zoya blurted. 'They've taken out the bridge.'

Cid's smile vanished, as Rosie put out an arm to stop the advance of the pirates behind her. 'Are they on board?' she asked.

'Not yet,' said Zoya. 'I don't think.'

'Where's Carlos?'

'Back there,' said Zoya, gesturing into the smoke. 'He sent me to get you.'

Rosie started issuing orders to the thieves behind her. As she did, Cid grabbed hold of Zoya. 'Is it the army? Where are they?'

'I don't know,' said Zoya. 'The missiles came from over there.' She gestured through the smoke to the patch of sky beyond the stern of the airship. Cid pulled up his goggles. After a moment, he ripped them from their cord and tossed them to the deck. 'Can't see a damn thing through this fog. Where the hell's the captain?'

'Here,' said Vaspine. He emerged from the smoke like a ghost, his clothes dusty and torn. 'They've smashed the bridge. We can't fly . . .'

Cid pushed past Vaspine. 'Let me see . . .'

The captain dragged him back. 'It's gone, Cid.'

Cid glanced at Vaspine to check he was telling the truth, then spun around and kicked his goggles across the deck. They flew through the air and thudded into the gunwale. 'Well, we can't just sit here while they shoot us to pieces,' he growled. 'Come up with a plan!'

No sooner had Cid finished than another projectile cannoned in from above. This one tore through a solar sail and its rigging, then diagonally down through the mainmast and gunwale. Above, the mast creaked loudly, made several sharp cracking sounds and dropped to the deck, bringing both sails down with it. The projectile had carved a wide gap in the gunwale. They watched it in silence, anxious looks on their faces, then groaned as the wood slowly flickered into flame.

'Rosie!' shouted Vaspine.

'Captain?'

'Have we still got those cannons from Dalmacia?'

Rosie nodded.

'Take five men and get them here.'

'They're already on their way.'

Vaspine smiled, but it faded almost immediately, as did that of every thief on the ship. To their left, beyond where the projectile had just landed, a hundred lanterns blinked into life, each casting a shadow and creating a web of light that sketched the outline of a giant airship. Zoya stared at the shape, amazed that it had managed to sneak so close without anyone noticing. Revealed by the light were the silhouettes of a hundred men.

To Zoya's left, Vaspine started to laugh—quietly at first, then louder. Cid cocked his head and stared at him. 'What the hell's going on? Is this some kind of joke?'

'Yes,' said Vaspine.

Ordinarily, when the captain let out a laugh, it was a sign that everything was OK. But there was something about this one—hysterical, almost manic—that chilled Zoya. Vaspine started to clap, then walked over to what remained of the gunwale. 'Come on,' he said, 'get out here you coward. Stop hiding.'

'That's a foolish thing to say to a man who holds your life in his hands,' said a voice from the dark. Zoya recognized it instantly, and glanced across at Bucker, a few paces away.

Lendon Kane.

Kane stepped out from the shadows and walked calmly to the front of his ship. He looked identical to when Zoya had last seen him falling to the ground from the back of the *Shadow*—no scars, no injuries. He was wearing the same black trousers, the same black waistcoat, moustache and top hat. The only difference, to Zoya's eye, was the blood-red shirt he wore in place of his usual white. The shirt shimmered a deep orange in the firelight.

'Hello friends,' he said, addressing the crew behind Vaspine. 'Judging by the looks on your faces, I presume you thought I was dead. Well . . .' he accompanied the next words with a wink, 'it takes more than a big fall to kill me.'

'How did you survive?' Vaspine snarled.

'You needn't worry about that,' said Kane. 'It won't have any influence on what happens today. I warned you not to inconvenience me. What kind of sky thief would I be if I put up with such an insult?'

'Rosie,' Vaspine said, his eyes still fixed on Kane, 'the ship's going down. Where are the chutes?'

'It's too late,' said Kane. 'Too late!' He shouted these last words so loud that even Vaspine quietened. 'Those earlier shots were a warm-up. Your airship is surrounded by three of mine. In a moment, I'm going to order them to obliterate you and everything on board. The woman, your pilot, the girl, the boy—you're all going to die.'

74

'Do it then,' snarled Vaspine. 'None of us want to hear you drone on.'

Kane smirked. 'They always said I had a taste for the dramatic. Still, I couldn't kill you without saying a personal goodbye to Zoya. Where is she?'

Zoya stepped forward before Rosie could stop her. Standing before him, her legs started to shake, but she was determined to hide it. 'Leave these people,' she said. 'I was the one who beat you. You only want me.'

'Not any more,' said Kane. 'I don't like being inconvenienced. Those who do this find they have a debt to pay. Like your friend. What was his name? Beebee?'

Cid rushed forward. 'Let me get my hands on that . . .' His words were cut short by the crack of a gunshot. The pilot dropped to the deck like a stone, blood seeping from his chest. As soon as Rosie realized what had happened, she bolted forward and dropped to her knees by his side, cradling his head in her hands.

'I wouldn't let it concern you.' Kane addressed Rosie from behind the barrel of his gun. 'It won't matter in a moment.' Kane whispered into the ear of a nearby pirate, who passed the message on to another behind him, who in turn flicked a match and set it to a dark shape above his head. The object—larger than a transporter—caught fire immediately. Zoya stared at it, unable to make out what it was, then she spotted the outline of a cannon. She sank to her knees.

'I suppose it's appropriate, you bowing,' said Kane. 'Especially when you're about to meet your maker. Just be sure to keep that locket safe. I'll be taking it off your dead body.'

Kane lifted his arm and dropped it to his waist. A roaring sound filled the air as the flaming object lurched upwards and out towards the *Dragonfly*. Simultaneously, half a dozen other projectiles exploded in flight, all centred on Zoya and her friends. The last thing Zoya saw before her world went black was a storm of orange fire.

15

From way down in the depths of darkness, Zoya heard a rustling. It was muted at first, but it grew louder as she started to stir, and more insistent until she realized it was coming from right in front of her face.

She opened her eyes.

A world of light flooded in, causing her to throw up her hands. In the snatches of illumination that filtered through her fingers, Zoya could see she was surrounded by green. *Where am I?*

A blaze of pain coursed through her temple. She shifted her hand to apply some pressure, and as she did her body swung beneath her. She glanced down and realized, with a skip of her heart, that she was hanging from a tree. Suppressing a wave of panic, she peered over her shoulder to see what was preventing her from falling. Her jacket— which she'd slipped on the previous night to protect her from the storm—had snagged on a branch, and was now the only thing between her and a fifteen-foot drop to the ground. Below, Zoya spotted some of the scattered remains of the *Dragonfly*—a few tables, a splintered section of the mainmast, a lump of the hull. Beyond this, the wreckage trailed off into the forest.

Slowly, she removed her hand from her forehead and wrapped it around a nearby branch. As she moved, Zoya heard a tearing sound behind her. But the jacket held. She didn't move again for a moment, simply hanging from the tree, listening to the birds and trying to figure out a way down. After a few seconds, she heard the rustling sound again. From out of the foliage to her left appeared a small monkey. The creature bounded effortlessly until it was a foot from her face. Plucking a leaf to nibble, it stared at Zoya— an almost sympathetic look in its eyes—before spying her jacket and stepping forward to investigate.

Zoya heard another ripping sound. 'Shoo,' she said. 'Shoo!'

The monkey froze at the sound of her voice and eyed Zoya suspiciously, before continuing. Zoya could feel the monkey's breath on her neck, but she didn't dare turn to look for fear of dislodging something important. 'Get away,' she said, through gritted teeth.

Her voice made the monkey screech this time, and it started to claw wildly, swiping at her neck and jacket. One swing severed a loose thread and caused Zoya to lurch down.

She shot a glance at the ground, then another up at the monkey, who'd bared his teeth in half-challenge, half-play. The monkey held her stare, then slashed the remaining threads of her jacket.

Zoya jerked downwards again, this time violently. The branch, around which she'd wrapped her hands, tore away and she started to tumble through the tree, clattering into branches with her head, arms, hands, feet. She thudded into the ground a moment later, winded by the impact. She lay in a heap on the floor, writhing in pain.

In time, the sensation passed and Zoya was able to breathe again. She pushed herself up. It was morning, not long after dawn. She looked up at the tree from which she'd fallen, the tattered remains of her jacket marking the height of her descent. How had she survived? How had she survived any of it—the fall, the flaming airship? She tried to remember what had happened, but everything after her conversation with Kane was a fiery, panicked mess. Images of scattered sky thieves, a burning ship.

Zoya shook away the thoughts and returned to the present. If she'd survived, there might be others. Ignoring the ache in her ankle, she staggered to her feet and surveyed her surroundings. She'd landed in a forest clearing about as wide as the deck of the *Dragonfly*. Scattered over the ground were the objects she'd spotted from up in the tree. She kicked aside a few barrels to see if there was anybody underneath. No luck. An urge to cry almost overwhelmed her, and she had to fight to maintain her calm. 'Come on,' she muttered. 'Come on.'

As far as Zoya could tell, she wasn't at the main crash-site. There just wasn't enough ship lying around. But she couldn't have fallen far if she'd survived, which meant she'd been flung from the ship shortly before it crashed. And that, in turn, was cause for hope. If she'd managed to hang on until such a low altitude, others could have too.

Zoya peered up into the trees that ringed the clearing and tried to work out the ship's trajectory. Sure enough, a deep, straight scar cut through the canopy. Zoya glanced around one last time to make sure there was nothing worth salvaging, then hobbled off in the direction of the scar.

She'd moved barely a dozen yards when she heard a groaning to her left, from behind a section of smashed hull. Zoya grabbed a length of the mainmast lying nearby, wedged it beneath the hull and tugged on the other end. Slowly, the wood lifted and toppled aside.

'Remind me to compliment your captain on his hospitality the next time I see him.'

Ahead of Zoya, a cage had landed at an angle. Sprawled inside was Dodsley Brown——his back flat against one set of bars and his legs up against the other.

'What are you doing?' asked Zoya.

'Enjoying the view,' said Dodsley. 'There's nothing like an

airship crash from inside a cage.' His face grew serious. 'Now, are you going to let me out?'

Zoya stared at Dodsley. Her head wanted to leave him in the cage, even if her heart said no. Before she could decide, she heard voices over her shoulder. The voices were faint, mumbling, but unmistakeable. Her first thought was one of joy. She wanted to run to them and see who'd survived. But then another thought occurred. What if the voices didn't belong to anyone from the *Dragonfly*? What if they were Kane's men? Or the Aviation Army?

Zoya shifted her weight onto her good foot, ready to run. Dodsley noticed her movement. 'Wait,' he said, a panicked edge to his voice. 'You can't leave me. I'm on the most-wanted list. If it's the Aviation Army, they'll throw me in prison for the rest of my life.'

Zoya raised an eyebrow.

'Zoya, please.'

'You should have thought of that before trying to steal the goggles.'

'They were *my* goggles,' snapped Dodsley, before he caught himself. 'Listen,' he said, adopting a quieter, friendly tone, 'if those voices belong to anyone but your friends, we're both in trouble. Now, I don't know how we've ended up down here, and I don't know why you're blaming me. But I do know this: I don't want to get caught. I also know that whoever they are,' he nodded in the direction of the voices, 'we're better off fighting them together.'

Dodsley stared at Zoya with pleading eyes. Zoya remained stationary, then sighed and stomped over to the cage. 'I need a wire,' she said, 'a thin one.'

Dodsley glanced at the shoulder of his coat. Poking out was a matchstick-sized metal splinter. 'That do?'

Zoya nodded. Dodsley gripped the end of the splinter with his teeth, then yanked his head. With the splinter between his teeth, he pushed his forehead up against the cage and dropped the scrap into Zoya's cupped hand.

'Go for it.'

Zoya shaped the wire so it would fit in the keyhole, then slotted it inside.

'C'mon,' said Dodsley.

'I'm doing it!' said Zoya.

Zoya's hands trembled, but after a few seconds she was able to trip the barrel and unhook the padlock, which dropped to the ground with a *thud*. For a moment, there was silence from the direction of the trees. Then the voices started up again, this time heading in Dodsley and Zoya's direction.

'Get it open,' whispered Zoya. 'Now!'

Dodsley pushed at the cage door, but it wouldn't budge. Zoya joined him, pulling as he pushed, but the door remained shut. The voices were so close now that Zoya could almost make out what they were saying. She figured they had a few more seconds before whoever it was emerged into the clearing. Zoya jumped away as Dodsley lay on his back and booted the door once, then twice—each kick making a dull clanging sound—until the third kick swung it open.

The voices were so close now that Zoya could hear the accompanying rustle of leaves as their owners stumbled through the last few bushes. Dodsley bolted from the cage, grabbed Zoya's hand and raced with her to the other side of the clearing. As they dived to the ground out of sight, four men rounded the corner into the clearing, each with a gun.

16

Zoya lay on the ground, her heart pounding so hard she had to remind herself the men wouldn't hear it. Dodsley put a hand on her shoulder as she pushed herself up just enough to sneak a look, but Zoya scowled and he took it away.

Now they were out in the open, Zoya could see the men for the first time. They weren't Aviation Army soldiers, that was for sure. Zoya had seen enough soldiers to recognize their uniform. Nor were they thieves from the *Dragonfly*. So they must be Kane's men. Zoya flushed hot with anger and fought the urge to charge them. But she remembered the guns just in time and sank back down.

'I definitely heard something,' said the shortest, a square-chinned man with a patch over his left eye.

'Don't be daft,' said another, this one's voice raspy, high-pitched. 'No-one could have survived the crash.'

'Yeah? Well, what are we doing here if no-one survived?'

'The boss wants to be sure.'

The men combed the area as they talked, kicking over anything big enough to conceal a person.

'He would send *us* to make sure,' said the first man again. He plonked himself down on an upturned barrel. 'Let's see him come down here and check himself. I notice he ain't taking any risks . . .'

The three standing stared at the one on the barrel. 'I'd watch my words if I were you. You wouldn't want that kind of talk getting back to Kane.'

A look of panic flashed across the small man's face. 'Easy now lads, it was a joke. You wouldn't tell him . . . ?'

'I will if you don't get off your backside and help us get this job done,' said high-pitch.

Zoya watched the small pirate. He lifted himself grumpily off the barrel and wandered absently in their direction, staring into the muzzle of his gun. He continued until he was a yard or so from the knoll behind which Zoya and Dodsley were hiding. The thieves stilled their breathing. Silently, Zoya reached for a length of the broken mainmast. A few agonizing seconds passed in which Kane's man studied the forest beyond the knoll. Then, as quickly as he'd arrived, he returned to the main group.

The raspy-voiced pirate smacked him around the back of his head when he returned. 'Nothing here, you dimwit. Let's get back to the main site before the Aviation Army gets there.'

The pirates took one last look around, then headed off into the forest, leaving Zoya and Dodsley in silence. Zoya held Dodsley down for a while, just to make sure Kane's men weren't tricking them. When they hadn't returned after another thirty seconds, she let him go and jumped to her feet. In an instant, Dodsley had vaulted the knoll and was running to the edge of the clearing.

'Oi!' hissed Zoya.

Dodsley wheeled around.

'Where are you going?'

'I'm gone,' said Dodsley. 'You think I'm sticking around for when those guys get back?'

Zoya smacked her hand to her forehead. 'Did you even hear what they said?'

Dodsley nodded.

'If you go that way, you're going to run straight into the Aviation Army.' Zoya held his stare, waiting to be called on her half-truth. In reality, she had no idea from which direction the Aviation Army would approach. Dodsley sighed hard as he thought. 'Besides,' continued Zoya. 'We'll do better together.'

'You might,' said Dodsley. 'I do best when I'm on my own.' He walked back towards Zoya as he considered what she'd said, then shook his head. 'OK, we walk together until we can both get away. Then I'm gone.'

'Fine by me,' said Zoya.

Before setting off, they each grabbed a weapon from the clearing——Zoya the shard of wood she'd brandished earlier, Dodsley a metal bar from the cage——then tramped into the forest. It was cold under the canopy. Zoya shivered and pulled her shirt close. Dodsley glanced down, then reluctantly removed his jacket and tossed it over. 'Thanks,' said Zoya, surprised.

'Just don't steal from the pockets,' said Dodsley.

They stopped every so often to listen for the men, but they seemed to have pushed far ahead. Without their voices to follow, Zoya tracked the scar in the trees. Sometimes they had to detour around standing water or a drop in the ground, but otherwise they walked unhindered. With each step, they stumbled upon more and more of the *Dragonfly*——each piece out of place in the forest. On one side of the trail, they encountered a bunch of bungee gear, then a spilled sack of potatoes, then one of the solar sail's metal frames. It was like a giant had plucked the airship from the sky and shaken it empty as he walked across the land.

Zoya froze.

From somewhere in the trees to her left she'd heard a noise. Dodsley heard it too, and he stared into the darkness, searching for its source. Zoya heard the noise again, this time behind her. She spun around and peered into the gloom. For some reason, the noise seemed familiar. It sounded like the birds Zoya and Beebee had played with back on the airship. Only . . . this was different. She waited quietly, and when the noise came again, she smiled. She relaxed her body and gestured for Dodsley to do the same. 'It's OK.'

'Zoya, is that you?' The voice came from somewhere amongst the trees.

'It's me, Bucker,' said Zoya. 'You can come out.'

Bucker emerged from the trees, his hair a mess of twigs and leaves, his clothes torn. Down the left side of his face ran a deep cut, clogged with dried blood. 'Are you OK?' she asked, hugging him.

'I've been better,' said Bucker. He looked up at Dodsley. 'What's he doing with you?'

'We're sticking together until we get out of here. Have you seen anyone else?'

'From the *Dragonfly*?'

'From anywhere.'

Bucker shrugged. 'There are some idiots going around with guns; I think they're Kane's guys. Otherwise, no.'

Zoya wrinkled her nose. 'No-one from the *Dragonfly*?'

Bucker shook his head.

'We've met the others,' said Zoya.

'I bet you didn't get one of these,' said Bucker. He pulled a gun from out of his trouser pocket.

Zoya smiled. 'Nice one.'

'I stole it from one of them when they walked past . . .'

Before Bucker could explain further, Dodsley snatched the weapon from his hand and started to inspect it in the

88

dim light of the forest. Bucker gestured for Zoya to get it back.

'Give it back,' she said, calmly.

Dodsley looked down. 'I'm the adult here. I keep it.'

'Well, we're the sky thieves,' said Zoya, mimicking his tone, 'and I say we keep it.' She leapt up to grab the weapon.

'Enough,' snapped Dodsley. 'You'll set it off.'

Zoya stopped reaching for it, but her look of fury remained.

'Listen,' said Dodsley. 'You sky thieves are all about swords and daggers, aren't you?'

Zoya nodded.

'Well, us city thieves, we're all about guns. In fact, I'd say I'm about the best shot in Dalmacia. So if you want to shoot yourself in the foot, take the gun. If not, leave it to someone who knows what they're doing.' Dodsley held out the gun for Zoya to take. She stared at it, then pushed it back.

'For now,' she said.

'So, what's the plan?' asked Bucker. 'Where is everyone?'

'We got thrown off the airship before it crashed,' said Zoya. 'I don't know.'

'Me too,' said Bucker. 'I woke up with my legs in a pond.' He pointed at his trousers, which were drenched.

'We overheard some of Kane's men say the airship was this way,' said Dodsley, 'so that's where we're going.'

Zoya nodded to confirm. 'We haven't got long. The Aviation Army will be here soon.'

The trees around them started to flatten as they hiked through the trench left by the falling ship. Ahead, the airship lay on its side, rising like a cliff-face. Parts of it had crumpled on impact, while others still smoked, unfurling black-grey spirals into the sky. Zoya walked alongside the craft, running her hand along its gunwale. Ahead, the mainmast had split in two, lying with what remained of the solar sails draped over it like a flag. Further along, the mess hall lay open, spilling food onto the ground.

Zoya started to search frantically amongst the smashed wood for survivors. She clambered all over the airship, desperate for a sign that somebody—*anybody*—had escaped. She searched every room, including those she knew Bucker and Dodsley had already checked. But no matter where Zoya looked, no matter how hard, she couldn't find anyone alive.

Outside, Zoya became aware of Bucker and Dodsley standing behind her. No one said anything. She felt a wave of sickness, and turned away from the others to throw up on the grass. She retched and retched until there was nothing left inside.

17

Zoya shuffled back to the front of the airship and dropped onto the upended gunwale. She sat, her head in her hands, until Bucker and Dodsley joined her. Together, they sat in a silence punctuated only by the crackle of nearby flames.

Eventually, Bucker spoke. 'Zoya, where are they?'

Zoya lifted her head. 'I don't know.'

'Are they dead?'

Zoya glanced up at Dodsley.

'O-Of course not,' said Dodsley. 'There are no bodies, for a start.' He thought for a moment. 'He's probably taken them prisoner. I mean, we survived, didn't we? Listen kids, there's lots of things in life to despair about, but this ain't one of them. If there's a chance your shipmates are alive, I'd hang onto it.'

Zoya was still furious with Dodsley, but she had to admit he was right on this one. There were no bodies. And if there were no bodies, that meant some of the crew might be alive.

She leapt up. 'Yes!' she said, shoving Bucker in the chest. 'He's right. We shouldn't give up. Would the captain give up? Or Cid?'

'No,' said Bucker.

'What about your mum?'

'Definitely not,' said Bucker.

'Then neither should we. We've been through worse. We beat Kane then and we'll beat him now.'

'But we've lost the airship,' said Bucker, slumping down. 'We can't beat anyone without an airship.'

'Then we'll get another,' said Zoya. 'Bigger.'

'And what if everyone's not alive?'

Zoya stepped over and placed a hand on Bucker's shoulder. Her voice was calm now, steeled. 'Then we'll go after Kane and make him pay.'

There was a moment's silence. Birds tweeted in the trees and small creatures scurried through the undergrowth. Then, suddenly, Dodsley started to back away, his eyes locked over Zoya's shoulder. 'Uh, Zoya, I don't think you're going to have to look far.'

Zoya whirled around. Entering the crash-site from the opposite side of the forest were Kane and his men—Kane stepping ahead like a king, tall and regal. When he spotted them, he pulled up, gesturing for his men to do the same. 'Well, well, well,' he said, 'it's my missing twosome.' He squinted into the sunlight. 'And unless I'm much mistaken,

92

that's my thief with them. What an interesting turn of events.'

'Where are they?' asked Zoya.

'Who?'

'You know.'

'Oh.' Kane smiled. 'Your crew-mates. I picked them up earlier. They'll be on their way to my fortress by now.'

'So they're alive?' said Zoya.

'Most,' said Kane. 'For now. That pilot of yours is in pretty bad shape. He'll need attention quickly, if he's going to make it.'

Zoya leapt towards Kane, her teeth bared. 'Where are they?'

'A-da-da,' said Kane, gesturing for his men to stand between them. 'That's not something you need to know. They're only alive because I hadn't yet found you. Now I have. And that locket of yours will finally be mine.'

The eight men flanking Kane started to advance, each pulling out their gun.

'Zoya,' shouted Bucker, 'get over here!'

Dodsley and Bucker had ducked behind a wall of potato sacks. Zoya took a last look at Kane, then leapt in behind them as the bullets started to fly. The projectiles slammed into the sacks, spraying pieces of potato in all directions. Zoya lifted her hands to protect her eyes, then leaned into Dodsley and nodded at his gun. 'How many bullets left?'

'Five,' said Dodsley.

'It's not enough.'

The bullets above their heads stopped briefly, and she took the chance to have a look. Kane's men were still advancing, reloading their weapons. They'd covered half the distance. Zoya ducked back down and elbowed Dodsley. 'Now!'

Dodsley leapt out of cover, fired three shots and dropped again.

'Did you get them?' asked Zoya.

'Two,' said Dodsley. 'But we need to get away.'

Zoya searched for a way to escape. Two options were available——the ship or the forest. Neither would work. Head into the ship and Kane would find them eventually. Head into the forest and they'd expose themselves to a wall of bullets. It was then that Zoya first noticed a noise in the background——a whirring drone. The crash-site had darkened too, as if a heavy cloud had blotted out the sun. Zoya glanced up to see a gigantic airship suspended in the sky. Attached to its side, fluttering in the breeze, was the burgundy emblem of the Aviation Army.

'Look,' said Zoya.

Dodsley and Bucker looked up as the bottom of the airship slid aside, revealing an enormous launch-bay. Emerging from this was a swarm of soldiers, and strapped to each of their backs was a contraption Zoya had never seen before.

Extending out of this was a black, metal bracket which rose above their heads and culminated in a pair of whirling copter blades. The blades spun in a circular blur, giving the soldiers enough lift to descend in a controlled manner. In their hands were weapons that they trained on Kane's men.

The men noticed the soldiers at the same time as Zoya, and turned to their boss for instructions. An irritated look flashed across Kane's face. He grabbed a gun from the nearest and started to fire at the soldiers. The others did the same, causing the Aviation Army soldiers to fire in return. Soon, the scene had turned into a blizzard of bullets, as the soldiers landed, discarded their backpacks, and raced for cover.

In the confusion, they had failed to see Zoya and the boys. 'What are those things?' asked Zoya.

'They call them copters,' said Dodsley. 'The Aviation Army just started using them.'

'Can they fly, or do they just drop?'

'I think they can fly. I've never used one though. Just going on what people have told me.'

'Do you see any other way out of this?' asked Zoya.

Dodsley shrugged.

'Buck, you good to give it a go?'

Bucker scoffed. 'I've bungeed off the side of an airship. I think I can deal with a little copter.'

'OK,' said Zoya. 'Those people you spoke to, Dodsley, did they mention how these things work?'

'Nope. But if it's like everything else in the Aviation Army, there'll only be one button. These things have to be numbskull-proof.'

'Sounds good,' said Zoya. 'We go on three. Run for the nearest copter. First one to work out how to make them go tells the others. We'll meet . . .' she paused, trying to think, then threw up her hands, '. . . somewhere in the sky. One, two . . .'

Bucker darted out from behind the sacks before Zoya could finish. Zoya and Dodsley followed. When they reached the copters, they dived to the ground. Squirming on the floor, Zoya manoeuvred so she was on top of a backpack, then hooked her arms into place. Without another touch, the backpack automatically tightened onto her back. She managed to turtle upright, then climb to her feet. Dodsley had made it up too, and was fiddling with a control panel on the front. Bucker was down. Zoya waddled over and offered him a hand. Once he was up, she turned to Dodsley. 'Have you got it?'

'I'm doing my best.'

Zoya glanced at her own control panel. Dodsley had been wrong in his prediction of one button, but there was one bigger than the rest. She pressed this and felt the copter blades spin above her head. Instead of lifting her up, the blades pushed her down, drilling her into the earth. Zoya yelped, and clawed at the panel for some kind of orientation control. Near her right armpit, she spotted a slider set to its lowest position. She tugged this up, and the copter started to accelerate into the sky. The airship above her grew quickly, until she could make out individual soldiers on its deck. Gripping the slider, she edged it down to its halfway point, slowing her ascent. But still she was travelling straight up, directly into the Aviation Army airship.

There must be a way to steer.

Zoya gripped the handlebars that jutted out in front and yanked them to the right, but the copter didn't move. She tried again, pulling harder. Still nothing. It was then that her fingers stumbled across a button on the end of the bar. She pressed it and heard a loud click above her head. The copter veered to the right. She reached down to her left, where she found another button. She pressed this one, and the copter veered to the left. Zoya smiled, and started to manipulate the buttons until she was straight.

A few feet away, Dodsley wrestled with the same problem. She watched him bring his copter under control, then turned her attention to finding Bucker. He wasn't in the sky around her, nor was he down at the crash-site or anywhere near the Aviation Army airship. She was just about to call his name, when a blurred shape zoomed quickly past her head. 'Wooohooo!' came the noise. 'This is amaaaaazzziinng!'

Zoya glanced up to see Bucker buzz across the sky as if he'd been flying copters all his life. When he knew he had her attention, he performed a couple of loops, an engine-stop, a drop, a restart, and he spun himself upside down. Zoya shook her head, but couldn't hide a smile.

On the ground, the battle between Kane's men and the Aviation Army soldiers continued. Now that the three of them were safe, Zoya exhaled. They'd ascended to a few hundred feet now. Bucker was above her and Dodsley a few yards ahead. Together, they drifted over dense forest, the crash-site—looking like a destroyed child's toy from the air—receding quickly. The forest ran for another few miles before breaking onto a narrow, rocky plateau. This curved away, so that Zoya could make out a cliff-face—its rocks rusty orange—tumbling off which was a majestic waterfall that emptied into a royal blue pool way below. Beside the lake were the squat houses and smoky wisps of a village, and beyond that, parked in a dusty stretch of land, a monorail. Two overhead rails issued from the station and soared into the distance, both decorated with glinting, jewel-like cars. Beyond, the view disintegrated into a shimmering smudge of land and sky. But Zoya knew where the monorail was heading. It was heading in the same direction everything went in that part of the world, a place where Zoya and Bucker would have to go if they wanted to find Kane's fortress and rescue the crew.

The city of Dalmacia.

18

They flew on in silence for a few minutes. In her head, Zoya tried to digest everything that had happened—Kane's return, the attack, the crash, the crew's disappearance. The air was cool and crisp, and the sun had emerged from behind the clouds. Small birds hovered nearby, fascinated by the novice fliers in their midst. Zoya shooed them away.

Bucker appeared to be enjoying himself, in spite of the crash. He pulsed the copter every now and then to gain a little lift, then dropped back into line. Zoya watched him out of the corner of her eye. He seemed genuinely content, oblivious that he might have lost his mother. She wanted to grab him, shake him, make him realize that if they failed to save her—if they failed to save all of them—Kane would kill them. But she didn't.

'I think we're safe now,' said Dodsley. 'There doesn't seem to be anyone coming after us.'

As Bucker buzzed up again, Zoya looked over her

shoulder. The Aviation Army airship was just a dot now, and what remained of the *Dragonfly* a speck in the forest below.

'I wonder if Kane got away,' said Dodsley.

'I reckon so,' said Zoya. 'He always does.'

'I should never have taken this job.'

'No,' said Zoya.

'It's not my kind of thing anyway,' said Dodsley. 'I don't normally work for violent people. But I needed the money.'

'Everyone needs money,' said Zoya. 'You shouldn't give up your morals.'

Zoya thought of Captain Vaspine, and everything he'd taught her. She felt a twinge of sadness.

'What was he talking about, the locket?'

Zoya glanced at Dodsley to see whether it was inquisitiveness asking, or the thief in him. She decided it was the former. 'That's why he came after us in the first place. I've got a locket that used to belong to Jupiter. It opens his vault.'

'*The* Jupiter?' said Dodsley.

Zoya nodded. She looked quickly at Bucker, unsure whether to say more. In the end, she decided to. 'He's my dad.'

Dodsley looked at her like she'd just claimed to have flown to the moon.

'It's true,' confirmed Bucker.

'*The* Jupiter?'

100

'Yes!' said Zoya.

Dodsley whistled. 'Can I see it?'

This was a question to which Zoya normally said no. Drawing attention to the locket was a bad idea. But there was something about Dodsley, some good in him. It echoed in his voice, radiated out of his smile. He might work for Kane, but he wasn't like the tyrant. She pulled the locket from around her neck and let it dangle loose. Dodsley leaned in to take a look.

'So last night was all about this?'

Zoya shook her head. 'He wants it, but I don't think that's it this time. There's not enough left in the vault to interest him. No,' Zoya kicked her boot into the sand, 'this is revenge. He wants to get back at me for destroying his ship.'

Dodsley raised an eyebrow. 'Not a man I'd like on my tail.'

'No,' said Zoya. They were approaching the edge of the forest now, the trees growing thinner and taller. 'Bucker, come here.'

Bucker was a few feet above. When he heard Zoya, he turned down the slider on his copter and dropped into place. 'What's up?'

'I think we should land on that outcrop and walk from there. We're too visible in the air. Sooner or later an Aviation Army airship's going to spot us, and if not them, then Kane. Agree?'

'Aww, but we're sky thieves,' he said, 'we fly. Besides, I'm enjoying this.'

'Bucker . . .'

'Whatever you think,' he said.

'Dodsley,' said Zoya, 'what about you?'

Dodsley jerked, surprised Zoya had asked him. 'Yeah, sure.'

They flew the last mile or so until they reached the border of the forest, then drifted gently to the ground. After shimmying out of their backpacks and concealing them under a nearby bush, they approached the edge of the plateau and peered down onto the desert sand. The cliff was a good mile high, overlooking an enormous stretch of land that ran all the way to the city. Dotted about its face were broad outcrops which people used for camping, judging by the charred fire-beds left behind. To the trio's left was the waterfall they'd seen from the sky, up which crawled a group of climbers, their ropes stretched to the top. A number of turbines were dug into the rock below these, providing power to a few wooden huts that sat on a nearby outcrop. From out of the huts ran wide conveyor belts that wound down the cliff and into the village below. 'Looks like some kind of quarry,' said Zoya.

'It is,' said Dodsley. 'The village is called Deeplake. Their rocks helped build the wall around the city. Even now they provide rocks to replace the ones where the wall is crumbling.'

'Have you been?' asked Bucker, tossing a stone over the edge and watching it fall.

'Once or twice,' said Dodsley. 'On jobs. I haven't been for a few years. Let's just say I have some . . .' he paused, grasping for the right words, '. . . unfinished business there.'

Zoya frowned. 'We need to go down there, get off the cliff.'

Dodsley stared at her. 'We?' he said. 'I said I'd come with you until it was safe for us to split. It's safe now. I need to get away from you two. Jupiter's daughter or not, you're bad news. You've got the Aviation Army after you. And Kane.'

'Don't you think Kane will be after you?' said Zoya. 'Now he's seen you with us?'

'Maybe.' Dodsley shrugged. 'But I'd rather take my chances.' He walked in the direction of the waterfall. Zoya looked at Bucker, who shrugged. But Zoya couldn't let it go. An anger started to boil inside her. She was furious at him for wanting to leave, and angry at herself for wanting him to stay. Losing control, she charged after Dodsley and tackled him to the ground. She pounded his back, fist over fist, until Bucker ran up and tugged her off. Dodsley rolled onto his back, flabbergasted. 'What are you doing?'

'It's you,' said Zoya, her eyes hot with tears. 'You caused all of this and now you're walking away. Don't you understand, we need your help? All of my family—everyone I know—

has been captured by that horrible man. We're scared. I'm scared. Bucker's scared. You've got to help us!'

There was an awkward silence, during which they exchanged glares. In the end, it was Bucker who spoke. 'Hang on Zo,' he said, 'it wasn't all Dodsley. You went to get the goggles. If you'd remembered Cid's birthday, you wouldn't have had to go in the first place. Besides, Kane was always going to come after you if he was alive. It was only a matter of time.'

Zoya shifted her glare to Bucker, but he held her gaze. Eventually, she looked away. Then it hit her. Bucker was right. All this time she'd blamed Dodsley for what had happened, when it was really her fault. She picked up a rock and hurled it to the ground. 'OK,' she said, 'it's my fault! But that doesn't change things. We still need to save them.'

Dodsley got up from the floor, brushed down his clothes, and walked to Zoya. 'Listen kid, this is no-one's fault but that maniac. Kane's the one who shot you and your friends down, and he's the one holding them now. There's nothing I can do to help you with that.'

'There is,' said Zoya. 'Look at what we've done so far. We've escaped Kane and the Aviation Army. We're good together. And if me and Bucker are ever going to see everyone again, we're going to need help.' She stared at Dodsley, who stood with his hands on his hips. 'Please, help us.'

104

Dodsley rubbed his chin and stared off into the distance. After a moment, he shook his head. 'Dammit girl, if you don't get me killed. I'll help you. I will. But we do what I say. I'll go with you to Dalmacia and help you get an airship, but after that you're on your own. I'm not going to Kane's den for all the gold in the world.'

A smile erupted on Zoya's and Bucker's faces. They ran up and hugged Dodsley. 'Thank you,' said Bucker. 'Thanks!'

'Don't thank me yet,' said Dodsley. 'You might come to regret it.'

'No,' said Zoya. 'We'll free them, I know we will.'

'Yeah,' said Dodsley.

'So, where's Dalmacia?' asked Bucker.

Dodsley pointed over their shoulders. Bucker and Zoya spun around and squinted into the distance. 'Where?' said Bucker.

'There,' said Dodsley. 'You're looking at her.'

Zoya looked again at the vista and realized that the hazy smudge she'd earlier taken to be a mix of sand and sky was actually the city wall. So high was the wall that it was impossible to see either over or around it. Beyond the monorail station, it filled her entire view. 'We're not far away,' said Zoya.

'It's further than you think,' said Dodsley. 'Fifty miles, give or take.'

Zoya slumped. 'Oh.'

'How do we get there?' asked Bucker.

'Slow down,' said Dodsley. 'We need to lie low for a bit first. The Aviation Army's going to have a bunch of ships looking for us in an hour or so. If we're not out of sight by then, we can kiss any rescue attempts goodbye.'

'Let's hide in one of the caves on the cliff,' said Zoya.

Dodsley gave her a look. 'The army's spent decades catching scumbags in these cliffs. What makes you think you can outsmart them?'

Zoya didn't have an answer. Dodsley approached the edge of the cliff and peered over. 'You see that?' he said, nodding down at the stairway cut into the stone. It started a few hundred yards to their right and wound down the cliff, spilling onto the canyon floor. 'If we walk down it, we can get to Deeplake in a couple of hours. God help me for saying this, but I know someone there who might take us in. If we're lucky and she's not still mad at me.'

'Sounds good,' said Zoya. 'This girl, though, what's she angry at you for?'

'Let's just say,' said Dodsley, backing away from the cliff-edge, 'when I see her she's either going to kiss me or kill me.'

With that, Dodsley stepped in the direction of the staircase, Bucker and Zoya following behind.

19

They emerged onto the cliff-face, blinking in the sun. The staircase was carved into the side of the cliff—a long, steep line of steps. According to Dodsley, the route had been a trade passage back in the days before airships, used by villagers beyond the forest to get their goods to the city. The steps were aligned so that the reddish-brown rock of the cliff-face remained to their left, and the vast expanse of the desert plain to their right. Each step was less than two yards wide, and sloped towards the cliff-face where countless people had worn the rock trying to avoid the edge.

Zoya did the same, glancing down into the desert every now and then to see how far they'd travelled. Bucker, alternatively, seemed to revel in the danger. He walked as near to the edge as he could, leaning over to get a better view, even lying on his belly and poking his head out so he could see directly down.

'You're going to fall off,' said Zoya.

'Have you ever seen me fall off anything?' asked Bucker.

Bucker skipped to the cliff-face, planted his foot into a chink in the rock, and did a somersault, landing easily on the other side of Zoya. She had to admit, he had the agility of a circus performer. But something about his attitude worried her. Since the crash, he'd barely said a word about his mum.

'He's fine, you know,' said Dodsley.

Zoya looked up. 'I never said he wasn't.'

'Your eyes did. You've got that worried look. But he's OK. Not everyone reacts to danger in the same way.'

Zoya glanced at Bucker, a few yards ahead, hopping from one foot to the other. 'Yeah, but he needs to be scared. I've seen what Kane can do.'

'We all have,' said Dodsley, silencing Zoya. 'Maybe he's got some faith in the people around him.'

Dodsley let the comment hang. It was mid-morning now, and very hot. The sun pounded the cliff-face, heavy and oppressive. A layer of fine dust built up on her skin, and she stopped every now and then to scrub her face with her palms.

One time, as she pulled her hands away, Zoya spied two men fifty yards further down the staircase. They were making their way up the steps, heavy packs on their backs. The men were rough-looking, with dirty clothes, tanned, creased foreheads and long beards. Zoya pointed them out to Dodsley, who shrugged and turned back to the horizon.

The men looked thirsty and exhausted. One glanced over his shoulder every few steps as if he was debating going back down.

Zoya rooted around in her satchel for some water. She figured the men probably needed it more than her. Besides, she reasoned, they'd be able to get more in Deeplake. And so it was that, as the men approached, Zoya stopped in the middle of the stairs. 'Hello. Would you like some water? We've got enough.'

No sooner had she spoken than Dodsley snapped his head round to glare at her. Even Bucker stopped. The men, too, seemed taken aback, and didn't immediately respond. The lower of the two looked over his shoulder, then nodded at the first. 'Yeah, that'd be kind,' he said. 'And I reckon I wouldn't mind having whatever's in that bag of yours as well.' He glanced at Zoya's neck. 'Oooh, and that chain.'

Zoya's eyes narrowed. 'That's not what I meant . . .'

Before she could finish, the first man had grabbed her by the throat and pushed her against the cliff-face. As he did, Dodsley and Bucker jumped forwards, but the second man stepped in to ward them off. The first man looked back to make sure they'd stopped, then leaned into Zoya. The man's hand on her throat—and his bad breath—nearly made her gag. 'Well,' he said, 'that is what *I* meant. And I suggest you do as you're told. You're a long way up here. All it would take is one little slip . . .'

Zoya looked at Dodsley, her eyes wide with panic. 'I suggest you let her go,' he said.

'Shut up,' said the first man.

'Last warning,' said Dodsley.

The man released Zoya's throat and faced Dodsley. He whipped a small dagger out of his belt and held it up ready to attack. Sensing the danger, Dodsley nudged Bucker behind him. 'Oh yeah,' said the man, 'and what are you going to do about it?'

A smile appeared on Dodsley's face. Before Zoya could work out what was happening, Dodsley had kicked the blocker down the staircase and leapt towards the one with the dagger. The man spotted the move too late and swept his blade down where Dodsley had been. Dodsley grabbed him and forced him up against the rock. 'If you ever touch her—or anyone like her—again, I will personally break your arm. Are we clear?'

The man nodded quickly. Dodsley eyeballed him briefly, then released his grip. The man stumbled up the mountain, coughing and spluttering. Dodsley raised a fist at the second man who was just getting to his feet, prompting him to spread his palms in submission and creep past.

Zoya and Bucker, a few steps below Dodsley, stared at him, open-mouthed.

'What?' asked Dodsley.

'Thank you,' said Zoya.

'That was insane!' said Bucker.

'Yeah,' said Zoya. 'That was cool.'

'Well,' said Dodsley, glaring at the men, 'I don't like it when people attack kids.' With that, he cracked his knuckles and walked on.

20

20

They reached the desert floor an hour later, tired and parched. The last step merged into a dust-path, which ran through baked ground to the village of Deeplake, a mile away. The village looked much larger now they were on the ground—a collection of squat, boxy buildings, with a clock tower rising above. Zoya glanced at the waterfall and lake, a sight unlike any she'd seen. She followed the water up the cliff. It looked like a length of silk—thinner at the top, thicker at the bottom.

A handful of boats bobbed gently near the lake's shore, and it was past these the path led on its way into town. 'Try to act naturally,' said Dodsley as they approached a group of sailors playing cards on the beach, 'like you live here.'

Zoya and Bucker did their best, sauntering along the path, nodding their greetings, saying hello if the chance occurred, reining in an urge to gawk at the waterfall. They followed the track around the lake until it met a gated entrance into town. Guarding the gate was an old man in a wooden booth, who appeared to have fallen asleep. As Dodsley approached, the man snorted, adjusted his position, then settled back down. Dodsley faced Zoya and Bucker. 'I guess we just go straight in.'

Deeplake's town square reminded Zoya of the one she used to sneak to whenever she wanted an afternoon away from the orphanage, with bustling market stalls, pedlars, street-entertainers, and hundreds of others going about their daily business. Overlooking the marketplace was a clock tower. At its foot was a sign: 'Welcome to Deeplake—an oasis in the desert'. Zoya walked up to the sign. 'Now what?'

'I need to have a wander,' said Dodsley, 'get my bearings. I can't quite remember where that girl's house is.'

Zoya and Bucker exchanged a glance. 'How do we know you're not going to run off?' asked Zoya.

'Or contact Kane and tell him where we are?' said Bucker. 'How do we know you're not still working with him?'

'You don't,' said Dodsley. 'You'll just have to trust me. Wait here until I come back.'

Dodsley slipped through the crowd. Zoya watched him until he disappeared, then turned back to Bucker, whose attention had already shifted to a large group across the street. Bucker had started to make his way across, and Zoya followed, slaloming through the lines of people queuing to buy groceries. The crowd comprised mostly mothers and children. Zoya was curious to see what was in the middle. Bucker must have felt the same, because he was already asking a nearby kid.

'He's the best in Deeplake,' said the kid. 'Go and have a look.'

Zoya and Bucker elbowed their way to the centre, where they found a young street-entertainer performing in front of a fountain. Despite his years, the kid sported a slim, blond moustache and had a strange habit of repeatedly blinking, giving him a constant look of anxiety. Zoya and Bucker watched him juggle balls, juggle knives, unicycle, then juggle knives and unicycle at the same time. Vaspine had once told Zoya that many sky thieves started their careers as street-performers, recruited by crew on visits to the surface. Seeing the boy, Zoya could understand.

After half an hour of collecting enough coins to fill his hat, the kid jumped down from his unicycle, hurriedly gathered his things and darted away into the crowd, bowing as he went. At first, Zoya couldn't understand why he'd left when he was making so much money. Then she spotted two uniformed soldiers from the Aviation Army's ground division strolling through the crowd, on patrol. Zoya pointed them out to Bucker, and together they sneaked to the other side of the street. Grabbing a couple of drinks in a café, they settled into seats outside and watched the soldiers closely. One was holding a piece of paper, and showing it to everyone he stopped, pointing at something on the sheet. Zoya had a nasty feeling it was her, Bucker, and Dodsley.

To Zoya's relief, Dodsley returned a minute later. She saw him from the café, standing on the spot at which he'd left them and scanning the crowd. Zoya hung back, waiting for the army soldiers to pass, then went over with Bucker. 'Dodsley,' she whispered.

'Oh, there you are,' he said. 'I was starting to get mad.'

'We need to get out of here,' said Zoya. 'There are a couple of soldiers.'

'I know,' said Dodsley. 'I saw them.'

'Have you found the place?'

'I think so. Come with me.'

Zoya followed Dodsley towards the clock tower. The crowd thinned, the further they got from the market, and pretty soon they were able to walk side-by-side. Dodsley led them down a narrow street, keeping in the shade of the overhanging houses. 'You never know who's watching.'

For the next five minutes, he led them through a labyrinth of alleys and side streets so complex that Zoya would have struggled to get them back to the main square if she'd tried.

'So, who's the girl?' asked Zoya.

'Be quiet,' said Dodsley. 'I'm trying to remember the way.'

The thief halted, going over the route in his head. In time, they turned into a new street, this one wider than the previous, lined with trees and bushes. One or two residences even had wagons parked outside, and Zoya was certain she spotted one with its own transporter. Dodsley led them halfway down, then stopped. 'This is it.'

He gestured at the house over his shoulder. Zoya peered at it as nonchalantly as she could, then back at Dodsley. 'OK, let's knock.'

'I already have,' said Dodsley. 'She's not in.'

'So we'll wait,' said Zoya.

'Not with those soldiers around and all these peeping eyes.' Dodsley pointed around them. 'No, we need to break in. We need to get around the back. Come on.'

Dodsley headed down an alley that bordered the house. Zoya glanced at Bucker, who shrugged. They caught up with the thief. 'I'm going to jump over the fence, then I'm going to pull you over. If you see anyone coming, shout.'

He vaulted onto a bin, then over the fence and down onto the other side. As he landed, Zoya heard a faint 'ouch.'

'Are you OK?' she whispered.

'Fine, fine,' said Dodsley. 'Is anyone coming?'

Zoya glanced at Bucker, who was positioned at the end of the alley. He shook his head. 'No.'

'Good. Send Bucker first.'

Zoya gestured for Bucker to approach, then gave him a boost. On the other side, Dodsley grabbed him and lowered him to the floor. When Zoya saw Dodsley's head reappear, she vaulted onto the fence, then allowed him to pull her over. She landed in a garden, one decidedly green for a dusty place like Deeplake. 'This is amazing,' she said. 'She must like plants.'

Dodsley nodded. 'She's got a lot of interests.'

The fence around the garden was tall enough so they could move without fear of being spotted. Dodsley led them to the back door—a big, oak barrier with a brass handle in its centre. Zoya searched nearby for a window to break—as only a battering ram would open the door—but there were none. 'Nice one,' she said to Dodsley. 'No wonder I got to the goggles first. You've got to be the worst thief I've ever met.'

Dodsley looked confused, then smiled. 'Oh, the door,' he said. 'Don't worry, I'll show you how we're going to get through there in a second. First, though, I feel I should tell you a little something about the lady who owns the house. She's . . . well,' Dodsley hesitated, 'well, she and I once had a thing. It didn't end well. The last time I saw her she threatened to kill me. So if she's a bit grumpy when she gets back and finds us in her house, you know why. Best leave the talking to me.'

Bucker looked up. 'What did you do?'

'You don't want to know.'

Dodsley shifted a small, leather knapsack he wore beneath his shirt around to his front and pulled out two glass vials, each the size of his finger. Dodsley arched his eyebrows at the kids, then carefully unscrewed the lid of the

117

first vial and poured a tiny amount of the powder onto the door handle. 'Abra . . .' He opened the second and poured a small amount of that on top of the first. He leaned over to a nearby bush and snapped off a stick about the length of his forearm. 'Stand back,' he grinned. ' . . . cadabra!'

Dodsley struck the handle with the stick, causing a small explosion. It wasn't loud—indeed, it was more of a *pop*— but it generated a lot of smoke. And when the smoke had cleared, Zoya realized that the door was swinging open. She looked at Bucker, whose mouth formed a surprised 'o.'

'See,' said Dodsley, taking a bow, 'you sky pirates might have your airships and your sword fighting, but us city thieves have our own tricks. Now let's go inside and wait, because I need a sit down.'

Dodsley hopped cheerfully up the step and into the house. As he did, a black metal poker connected squarely with his forehead. He remained still for a moment, shook his head once, then dropped to the floor. Where he'd been standing was a woman, about the same age as Dodsley. She looked out of her doorway at the kids. 'My name is Eva Hart,' she said, 'and this is my house. You've got about two seconds to tell me your names before you follow your friend.'

21

'Well, come on, out with it,' said Eva, as Zoya and Bucker stood dumbfounded.

'My name's Zoya,' said Zoya. 'This is Bucker.'

'OK,' said Eva. 'And what the hell are you doing breaking into my house?'

Zoya tried to think of an excuse that would sound genuine, but sighed. 'You wouldn't believe us if we told you.' She nodded down at Dodsley, still unconscious. 'Dodsley said you'd take us in for the night. That's all.'

Eva cocked her head, the poker still aimed at Zoya and Bucker. 'What did you say?'

'I said you wouldn't believe us.'

'No, the other bit.'

'Dodsley.'

Eva stared at the crumpled heap on the floor, then dropped to her knees. With one hand still clutching the poker, she used the other to roll Dodsley onto his front and angle his face so it caught the light. 'Oh dear,' she said. She looked up at Zoya. 'You, there's a towel in the cupboard. Soak it with water and bring it to me. And you,' she pointed her poker at Bucker, 'there's a mat in the front room. Bring it here.'

Bucker stepped into the house as Eva lowered the poker and laid it on the floor. Zoya followed a moment later. A part of her was tempted to dive at the poker and use it against the girl. But somehow Eva didn't seem like a threat any more. All the aggression had seeped away. Instead, Zoya wandered through to the cupboard, grabbed the towel, drenched it under the kitchen tap and took it back to Eva. 'Where is he with the mat?' she asked.

Bucker returned after a few seconds and unfurled the mat on the floor. Together, they lifted Dodsley onto it and Eva laid the towel across his forehead. 'Well, I did say I'd kill you the next time I saw you,' she muttered.

'Is he OK?' asked Zoya.

'He's fine,' said Eva. 'He'll come around in a minute. You really shouldn't go breaking into other people's houses like that. This is what happens.'

'We didn't think you were in,' said Zoya.

Eva arched her eyebrows, then let them drop. 'Go and open that window, would you? Let some air in.'

Zoya padded to the window and pulled back the curtains. For the first time, she was able to see Eva properly. She was slim, almost as tall as Dodsley. Her hair was the colour of autumn leaves—a mix of oranges, browns, and reds—which she wore high in a ponytail, stray wisps curling onto her cheeks. Her clothes were reminiscent of Zoya's—a brown leather waistcoat over a white shirt (sleeves rolled to the forearm) and a pair of brown shorts. Strapped to each leg was a belt, off which hung a number of items—gun holsters, daggers, and what looked like a money pouch—and below these stood a pair of knee-high boots, decorated with brass dragons. However, outshining all of this—to Zoya, at least—was a pendant around Eva's neck. Even though it was obscured by her shirt, there was something familiar about the necklace, something that reminded Zoya of her own. She wanted to walk up to Eva and pull out the chain to take a look.

If Eva was a thief like Dodsley, she was unlike any Zoya had met. All the female sky thieves on the *Dragonfly* had a boring, functional sense of fashion. Eva was different. Eva had style.

'Fill up that glass and bring it here. I think we need to speed up this waking process.'

Eva winked at Zoya, who picked up the glass and filled it with water. 'Would anyone else care to do this?' asked Eva. 'If he annoys you as much as he annoys me, I'm sure there'll be a queue.' She glanced between Zoya and Bucker. Both smiled, but shook their heads. 'OK. But you're missing the chance of a lifetime.'

Eva tossed the water directly into Dodsley's face, causing him to sit bolt upright, eyes wide. 'Wha . . .?'

'Hello,' said Eva.

'Eva,' mumbled Dodsley. 'What happene . . .'

'You tried to break into my house.'

Dodsley lifted his hand to his forehead and rubbed at the bruise that was starting to form. 'Did you hit me?'

'Yes,' said Eva. 'And I'll hit anyone else who enters my house without ringing the bell.'

'We thought you were ou . . .'

'I know,' said Eva, 'you thought I was out. But I wasn't. And this is the price you pay.' She extended a hand and helped him to his feet. 'But no harm done. Now, you three look like you haven't showered or eaten for a while. Why don't you clean yourselves up? I'll put some food on and you can tell me what's going on.'

Dodsley stared at her, confused. 'Aren't you angry?'

Eva laughed. 'Oh, I'm furious.' She nodded to emphasise her point. 'But that'll have to wait, I think.' She held Dodsley's stare until he nodded in recognition, then turned away.

For the next hour, Eva made Zoya and Bucker feel like they were back on the airship. She gave each of them a fresh towel and showed them to the bathroom. Zoya remained in the bath for longer than she ever had, giving the water time to draw the dust from her skin. When she finally got out, the water was a grey mess. She dried herself off, then headed downstairs to find Eva frying some onions ready for a stew. 'Do you need a hand?' she asked.

122

'Can you cook?'

'Not really.'

'Well, then,' Eva thought for a moment, 'you can chop.'

She stationed Zoya at the end of the bench with a wooden chopping board and sharp knife and asked her to peel and slice carrots, broccoli, cabbage, garlic, and a bunch of other vegetables Zoya had never seen before. At the other end of the worktop she had Dodsley chopping chicken into pieces, which she fried in butter along with the onions.

'How do you two know each other?' asked Zoya, when the stew was bubbling away. Dodsley was just about to answer, but Eva lifted her head out of the pan and smiled.

'I think we should save talking for the table. Where's Bucker, anyway?'

Zoya peeked over her shoulder. Bucker was standing at the side of the room, gazing up at the ships-in-bottles on Eva's wall. 'I'm here,' he said.

'There are a bunch of knives and forks in the drawer over there,' said Eva, gesturing with a spoon. 'Set them on the table, and fill that jug with water. Glasses are in the cupboard.'

Bucker tore himself away from the ships and did as he was told. Eva handed Zoya the final job of stirring the stew while she carved a loaf of bread into thick chunks and laid them in a basket in the centre of the table. This done, she grabbed the pan and ladled the stew directly into bowls at the table. The food smelled incredible, and Zoya was happy when Eva filled the bowls all the way to the top, the liquid oozing onto the tablecloth. 'First we eat,' said Eva, laying the pan in the sink, 'then we talk.'

She didn't have to tell them twice. They dived into the food like they hadn't eaten for a week. Zoya finished her bowl in less than five minutes, broke off chunks of bread and used them to soak up the stew that clung to the bottom. Eva ate slowly, chewing her food and watching them.

When they were finished, Eva removed their bowls to the sink, refilled their glasses, and sat back down. 'OK,' she said. 'Now you can tell me what's going on.'

Zoya and Dodsley shared a glance, then Zoya nodded for Dodsley to speak. Dodsley spent the next few minutes explaining to Eva everything that had happened—the chase at the museum, his imprisonment, the airship crash, Zoya's rescue, their escape from Kane and the Aviation Army, their descent down the cliff, the attack by the two men, and finally their breaking into her house. Eva listened intently, her head on her hands and her eyes fixed on Dodsley.

When Dodsley had finished, he looked at the kids to make sure he'd included everything, then reclined in his chair. Eva took a couple of deep breaths. 'If you're double-crossing them Dodsley Brown, I will come after you and throw you off the top of the cliff.'

Dodsley threw out his palms, hurt. 'I'm . . . of course I'm not.'

Eva flicked her eyes to Zoya. 'I presume you think the Aviation Army's still after you and you want to lie low here for the night. Is that right?'

'They're definitely after us,' said Zoya. 'We saw two soldiers asking around town.'

'Do you know how much trouble I could get into for harbouring fugitives? They'll send me straight to jail.'

'I know,' said Dodsley. 'I wouldn't have come if we weren't desperate.'

'You could have stayed at an inn,' said Eva.

Dodsley arched his eyebrows. 'That's the first place they'd look.'

Eva shrugged.

'Listen,' said Zoya, cutting in, 'if it's too much trouble, tell us. We're grateful for the meal, aren't we?' She kicked Dodsley and Bucker under the table, both of whom nodded. 'But we can get out of here. I don't know where we'd go, but we can leave. But if you can let us stay, that would be amazing. And when all of this is over, and we're back with the airship, I'll make sure we repay you.'

Eva rolled her eyes. 'I'm not looking for payment.' She stared at Dodsley. 'At least not from you, Zoya.'

'So we can stay?'

'Of course.'

'Thank you thank you thank you,' said Zoya. She jumped up from her seat and gave Eva a kiss.

'It's fine,' said Eva. 'To be honest, any chance to stick one to the Aviation Army is good by me. But tell me something, what's your plan? What are you going to do when you leave?'

Zoya's face soured. 'I don't know,' she said. 'We've not thought about it.'

'Well, you'd better,' said Eva. 'Because the Aviation Army doesn't give up easily. And neither will Kane, I bet.'

There was a moment's silence as they considered what she'd said, then Bucker lifted his head. 'We're going to rescue them.'

Eva smiled. 'I know that. But how? You don't even know where this man's taken them.'

'We'll go to Dalmacia,' said Dodsley. 'Someone there will know.'

Eva wrinkled her nose. 'You'll have to be careful. Dalmacia's swarming with informants and any number of people who'd happily shop you for a reward.'

Dodsley tried to act offended, then accepted her reasoning.

Eva sighed. 'I think I need some time to think all this through. Zoya, would you help me with the dishes?'

'Of course.'

'Boys,' said Eva, 'there are a few logs under the stairs. Take them out back and chop them up ready for a fire. There's an axe near the shed.'

Bucker and Dodsley disappeared out the back. Eva and Zoya cleared away the rest of the plates, then watched the boys through the window as they washed up. 'It's not often you see a girl your age up with the sky thieves,' said Eva.

'It's a long story,' said Zoya.

Eva took the hint. 'Another time, then.'

'Yeah,' said Zoya. 'What about you, anyway?'

'Me? What do you want to know?'

'Like, how do you know Dodsley?'

'Oooh,' said Eva, drying a pan and putting it back in the cupboard, 'that's not a good question if you want to get to bed tonight.'

'OK.'

'I'm joking.' Eva smiled. 'You really are wound up tight at the minute, aren't you?'

'It's been a long day.'

'You'll rescue them,' said Eva, resting a hand on Zoya's shoulder. 'The bad guy never wins for long.'

Zoya sat down as Eva put away the last of the plates. 'How about a hot chocolate? You look like you could do with it.' Zoya nodded. Eva set the milk on the hob, selected two mugs, broke into them a few chunks of chocolate, and added sugar. 'I've known Dodsley since we were your age,' she said, crushing the mixture with the end of a spoon. 'We were street kids in Dalmacia. I used to see him around, working cons or pickpocketing people in the main square. Then one night we both got arrested and the Aviation Army soldiers tied us together in the back of a transporter. That's where it all started.'

'I can't imagine Dodsley when he was young,' said Zoya. 'What was he like?'

'Oh, a real firework. As handsome as he is now. I liked him from the start. That night, we managed to escape from the transporter. He cut the ropes with a little penknife and we jumped out the back before it even took off. After that, we stuck together. He looked after me, taught me all about stealing——where to get jobs, tricks, techniques, who to sell to, everything. It wasn't long before we could afford a small place in Dalmacia. Nothing special, of course. Not like here. But it was ours. We carried on robbing to fund it, we became quite a team.'

Eva removed the pan from the hob, poured milk into the mugs and stirred. When they were ready, she brought them over to the table and set one in front of Zoya.

'So, why did you say you wanted to kill him?'

Eva sighed. 'My idea of being part of a team and his were very different.'

'How come?'

Eva smiled. 'Now that is a question for another time.'

'OK,' said Zoya. 'But if you don't mind me asking, how did you end up in Deeplake if you used to live in Dalmacia?'

'A clean start,' said Eva, blowing on her chocolate and taking a sip. 'Things got a little rough in Dalmacia. The Aviation Army were after me for a robbery and they weren't giving up. I tried to give them the run-around. I moved, I changed names, but they kept coming. So I took that as a sign to get out.'

'I can't believe you were a thief,' said Zoya. 'You seem so . . . normal.'

'There's nothing wrong with being a thief,' said Eva, offended. 'You of all people should know that.'

'I know,' said Zoya. 'I just mean, this house is so . . .'

'Plain?'

Zoya nodded.

'Sometimes you have to be plain to fit in,' said Eva.

'What do you do here?'

'I don't rob any more,' said Eva. She'd finished her chocolate now. She took the mug to the sink and ran it under some water. 'I got a job up at the waterfall breaking rocks. It's boring, but it pays OK.'

'You work in the quarry?'

Eva giggled. 'You don't have to be surprised. I'm not a grandma!'

Zoya smiled. 'It's just . . .'

'I know,' said Eva. 'It's a quiet life, but that's the way it's got to be.' She walked to the airships-in-bottles. 'I spend most of my time doing these now, and taking walks down by the lake. It's beautiful down there. If you're ever here again, you should take a walk along the beach.'

'I will,' said Zoya.

There was a click at the back door, then it swung open

and the boys stepped inside, a bunch of logs under their arms. Eva smiled. 'I think our men have done a good job out there.' She winked at Zoya. 'I suppose there's a first time for everything.'

Dodsley mimicked her as she spoke.

'Listen,' said Eva, ignoring him, 'I don't know about you guys, but I feel like doing something to take our minds off all this doom and gloom. Anyone fancy a game of cards?'

'That's the best idea anyone's had all day,' said Bucker.

22

They played cards late into the night. Zoya and Bucker won every game, just like they always had on the *Dragonfly*. Eventually, sleep overcame them all and one-by-one they drifted off to bed. Zoya slept in the front room beneath the card table, with a blanket and a pillow from Eva's bed. In the morning, she woke early to find the sun filtering through the curtains onto her face. Judging by the quiet, everyone else was still asleep. Zoya didn't want to wake them—they all needed a good night's rest—but she didn't want to sit around either. Instead, she pulled on her clothes, swung a hood over her head, and slipped out the back door.

It was chilly outside, even in the sun. A crisp, icy breeze blew across town, causing Zoya to shiver. Eva had lent her a jacket the night before, and Zoya pulled this close now, lifting the collar to shield her neck. She vaulted over the fence and into the alley. From there, she navigated back to the edge of town, towards the lake.

The lakeside was empty when she arrived. It reminded Zoya of early lookout shifts on the *Dragonfly*, when the deck was peaceful and quiet and there was just her and the sky. Zoya threaded her way to the shore, listening to the creaking of the boats. An early morning mist drifted across the water, and the sunlight twinkled off its surface, each point shining like a star against the blue. Beyond, the water frothed white, stirred by the torrent above.

Zoya liked being one of Vaspine's sky thieves—the robberies, the excitement, the sense that she was doing good—but she could understand how one might trade it all for a tranquil life next to the lake. Maybe one day she could live in a village like Deeplake—change her name, get rid of the locket, hide from the Aviation Army and Kane and everything. Live peacefully.

'What are you doing here?'

Zoya jumped up, ready to run.

'It's OK,' said Eva, approaching. 'It's me.'

Zoya let go of her breath. 'Don't do that! I thought you were the army!'

'Not unless they make soldiers out of ex-thieves.'

Zoya smiled. 'I woke up early, thought I'd come down.'

'Well,' said Eva, 'I've just been for a run and I spotted a bunch of Aviation Army soldiers camped beyond those bushes. They know you're in town. We need to get back.'

Zoya's pleasant thoughts receded rapidly. She followed Eva along the path back to the village, then through the winding streets to her house. When they arrived, Bucker and Dodsley were already awake, frying some leftover chicken and brewing coffee.

'They're here,' said Eva, bursting into the kitchen. Dodsley let go of the frying pan immediately and crossed the room to his knapsack, but Eva caught his arm as he passed. 'Down by the lake. We have time.'

'We need to get out,' said Bucker.

'I agree,' said Zoya.

'First, you need to eat,' said Eva. 'Then you need to think. They're going to be doing door-to-doors, so it'll take them a while to get this side of town. That's also going to make it a lot more difficult to get away. They'll have checkpoints on the road to the monorail station at least, probably further.'

'Then we'll head into the country,' said Dodsley.

'It's the Aviation Army,' said Eva. 'Don't you think they can spot a couple of people from the sky?'

The question silenced them. They finished preparing breakfast, then laid it on the table and helped themselves. 'The way I see it,' said Eva, 'you're going to need an airship, wherever Kane's taken your friends. Am I right?'

Zoya nodded.

'Well, the only place you're going to get one is Dalmacia. There's nothing big enough in Deeplake.' Eva took a breath. 'Listen, I know a guy there, a man I worked for after you left.' She looked at Dodsley. 'He taught me how to fly.'

'Will he lend us a ship?'

Eva grimaced. 'Not exactly. But . . .'

'So, we steal it?' said Dodsley.

Eva downed the last of her coffee. 'Well, he does owe me money.'

'But he doesn't owe us money,' said Dodsley.

'That's where I've been thinking,' said Eva. 'What would you say if I came with you?'

The others turned their heads. 'What?'

'Two kids and one buffoon,' she looked at Dodsley as she said this last. 'You're not going to be able to do this on your own. Not only have you got to get a ship, you've somehow got to find out where Kane's keeping your friends and then how to spring them. You just won't be able to do that without me. Hell, I'll bet none of you can even fly an airship.'

Zoya and Bucker looked at each other and shrugged. She had a point.

'And these people are worth it, right?' continued Eva. 'They're good people? You're not setting out to rescue any murderers, are you?'

Zoya and Bucker shook their heads. 'No way!'

'The way I see it,' said Eva, rising from her seat to shift the plates to the sink, 'I've got to go.'

'You can't though,' said Zoya. 'You're happy here.'

'Happy?' Eva regarded Zoya as if she'd lost her mind. 'These last few years have been the most boring of my life!

Ever since this dope left me in the lurch, I've been dreaming of a chance like this, something to get me back in the game. And here you guys are, turning up on my doorstep. It's fate!'

Zoya, Bucker, and Dodsley looked at each other. Eventually, Zoya turned to Eva. 'Well, thank you,' she said. 'But you know Kane, he's a dangerous man.'

'He's not the first I've met.'

'In which case,' said Zoya, smiling, 'thank you!' She leapt out of her seat and threw her arms around Eva. Bucker did the same. 'We're going to go and get my friends. And then I'll get Captain Vaspine to give you a place on the ship, and you can meet Rosie and Cid!'

'Easy,' said Eva, gently pushing them away, 'one thing at a time. First, we need to get out of this city without the Aviation Army catching us. That's going to be tricky, but I think I've got a plan. I'll tell you on the way. But for now, we need to get ready. I want everyone packed and back in this room in ten minutes.'

Zoya and Bucker smiled, then nodded and disappeared into the front room to grab their things. Dodsley pushed himself off the table and laid a hand on Eva's forearm. 'Thank you.'

'It's not for you,' she said. 'I can't leave them alone with you. God knows the trouble you'd get them into.'

Dodsley frowned. 'I know,' he said. 'That's why I'm thanking you.'

23

Ten minutes later, Eva crept cautiously into the street to check whether the Aviation Army were already there. Zoya followed once Eva gave her the all-clear, a new dagger strapped to her side. Bucker exited next, a smile on his face, happy to be moving. Last came Dodsley, blinking in the sun. Eva led them out of her street, towards the town square.

'Hang on,' said Zoya. 'Why are we heading to town?'

'If we try to walk past the checkpoint, they're going to find us. So we're going to sneak past instead.'

'Yes, but why go into the centre? That's where all the soldiers are, surely?'

'I think I know,' said Dodsley.

They'd left the tree-lined streets of Eva's district now and were entering the dustier streets downtown. The road on which they walked was lined with tall houses, sandy in colour and weathered in places, revealing the brickwork underneath. Nestled amongst these were grocers and cafés, their fronts busy with people shopping for the day's meals. It was into one of these shops that Eva guided them, whispering for them to blend in. Eva waited outside, keeping an eye on the street. Zoya watched as best she could from inside, and felt herself stiffen when she saw the bulk of four Aviation Army soldiers appear around the corner. It looked as if they were heading for the shop, but before they could get inside, Eva stepped forward.

'Someone suspicious?' Zoya heard the soldier say through the door. 'Down there?'

'I don't know about suspicious,' said Eva. 'But I've not seen them around before.'

The soldiers exchanged a glance. 'Well, thank you,' said one. 'If you see them again and we're not nearby, make sure you tell someone in burgundy.' The soldier nodded at his uniform, its eagle crest shining.

'I will,' said Eva. She watched the men hurry off in the direction she'd given, then gestured for the others to come out.

Dodsley tapped his head. 'I see you've still got it.'

'It's my honest face!' Eva winked.

They reached the square a few minutes later, and immediately entered Zoya's café from the day before to lie low. From their table, they had a clear view of the market stalls. Parked at their rear was an Aviation Army transporter, around which milled a handful of soldiers, chatting and joking. Zoya watched them out of the corner of her eye. There had to be at least half a dozen, excluding those already prowling the stalls with 'Wanted' posters. On the other side of the square, four quarry wagons were parked next to the dust road that led out of the town, their drivers waiting for cargo. 'What time do they normally set off?' asked Zoya.

'The rocks should arrive in a few minutes,' said Eva. 'Don't worry, everything's going to be fine.'

But Zoya did worry. If the Aviation Army soldiers found her, she'd never be able to rescue Vaspine, or Cid or Rosie or any of the rest of the crew. She fought the urge to jump up and run, until she spotted a caravan of wagons trundling in from the direction of the waterfall. 'Look,' she said.

'Ah,' said Eva. 'That's what we've been waiting for.'

The caravan bounced and jolted along the uneven road, through the centre of the market and pulled up behind the parked wagons. Seeing the new arrivals, the snoozing wagon drivers jerked awake and started to unload the rocks from the back of the caravan-wagons into their own.

'How're we going to get in without them seeing us?' asked Bucker.

A look of puzzlement appeared on Eva's face. 'To be honest, this is as far as I've thought. I guess we need to cause a distraction.'

Zoya fidgeted in her seat. The longer they stayed in the café, the more likely it was that someone would recognize them. She searched for something to use as a distraction. There were dozens of people around now, but involving one of them would be risky. What if they decided to alert the soldiers? From out of the corner of her eye, Zoya noticed something move in the clock tower. She flicked her eyes up and peered into the shadows. Her mind jumped to all sorts of conclusions—was it some kind of Aviation Army spotter, or one of their crack snipers? She shook such thoughts from her head and focussed on the wooden beam that ran horizontally below the clock-face. Creeping across the beam, pausing every now and then to lick its paw, was a kitten. Zoya's mind started to churn. An idea started to form. She turned to Bucker. 'Fancy a bit of acting, Buck?'

'What?' he asked, setting down his drink.

'Are you feeling brave?'

'Brave enough.'

Zoya turned in her seat and pointed up to the cat. The others craned their necks to follow the line of her gaze. The cat was still perched on the crossbar, a few yards below the clock.

'Oh no,' said Eva, quickly understanding Zoya's plan. 'It's too risky.'

'Bucker can do it, I know he can.'

'Do what?' asked Bucker, glancing at Dodsley.

'No.' Eva shook her head. 'If one of us gets caught, we all do.'

'Get caught doing what?' asked Bucker.

Zoya took a breath. 'We need to create a diversion, like Eva said. We can't ask anyone here to do it in case they shop us. That means we've got to do it. I was thinking you could run up to them and pretend the cat's yours. Ask the soldiers to get it down. While they're busy with that, we'll jump into the back of the wagon.'

'You want me to run right up to the soldiers?'

Zoya cringed. 'Not right up, but close enough so they can hear you.'

'To them?' said Bucker, jerking his thumb over his shoulder.

Zoya nodded. 'Listen, we take this one risk and if it works we get the soldiers out of our hair for good.' She glanced at the others for agreement. Dodsley shrugged, Bucker frowned, and Eva smiled awkwardly. 'Has anyone got a better idea?' asked Zoya. When there was no response, she sat forward. 'C'mon Bucker, we've done stuff like this before. You're good at it!'

Bucker rolled his eyes. 'OK,' he said. 'What do I do?'

'Yes,' said Zoya. 'Right, you need to walk up to the soldiers and shout that your cat's up on the clock tower. Do it loud, don't be scared. Make sure everyone in the square hears you. And you've got to sound worried. When everyone looks up, run back to the wagons. We'll meet you there.'

'What if they recognize me?'

Zoya pursed her lips, deep in thought. After a moment, she lunged forwards, ruffled Bucker's hair so that it fell in straggles across his face, scrunched up his clothes, ripped a hole in his shirt and undid the top two buttons. 'Now you look like a street urchin,' she said. 'They won't think you're anything!'

Bucker looked at himself. 'OK,' he said. 'OK, I'll do it.' He rose from his seat and started to walk away.

'Buck?' said Zoya.

He spun around.

'Get it right.'

Bucker nodded, then slid purposefully through the crowd towards the soldiers. He kept his eye on the cat with each step, making sure it remained still. When he arrived, he turned back to the café, smiled a cheeky grin, then wheeled around, pointed up to the clock tower and yelled, 'My cat, my cat! Up there! My cat!'

At first, nobody responded. But when Bucker repeated his shout, this time grabbing the forearms of passers-by and directing them up to the tower, one or two people started to look. Pretty soon, others followed, then the soldiers, the wagon drivers, the stall owners, and eventually the entire square.

The others took their chance, making their way stealthily to the back of the nearest quarry wagon. Peeling back the fabric cover that held down the rocks, Dodsley glanced around to check the way was clear, then boosted Zoya and Eva inside before jumping in. Bucker arrived a moment later, pausing beside the wagon to observe the chaos he'd caused—the Aviation Army soldiers fighting to be the first to rescue the cat—before he, too, scrambled over the lip of the wagon and into the darkness.

24

They lay breathless beneath the blanket, listening to the sounds in the square as the soldiers first tried to reach the cat with a ladder, before resorting to climbing the clock tower itself. They could tell the cat had finally been rescued when they heard a mighty cheer go up from the crowd, then listened to it fade as the soldiers realized Bucker was missing. 'They're going to get suspicious now,' whispered Eva. 'Let's hope the driver gets out of here soon.'

Zoya's heart beat rapidly when she heard footsteps approach the driver's cabin.

'I think that's our guy,' said Dodsley.

'It'd better be,' said Bucker.

The wagon jolted as the driver started the engine, then began to rumble beneath them, causing the loose rocks on which they were lying to judder. Zoya heard the driver say his goodbyes, then felt the wagon pull away. A smile blossomed on her face. 'I think we're getting away with it,' she whispered.

'That was the easy bit,' said Eva. 'We've still got to get past the checkpoint.'

Zoya slumped down on the rocks. In the rush to escape, she'd forgotten all about the checkpoints outside the village. If the army were in Deeplake for them, they were certain to search every vehicle leaving town. 'We might have to fight,' she said.

'That's the conclusion I've come to,' said Eva. There was a moment's silence before she spoke again. 'Everyone, check your weapons.'

A quiet rustling emanated from the back of the wagon as they each felt for something to fight with. Zoya snaked a hand down her leg and gripped the dagger Eva had given her. The wagon rumbled along for another few minutes, its rocks digging into Zoya every time the vehicle bounced, then she heard the whistling of the driver stop abruptly, and felt the wagon slow down. 'What's going on?' Zoya heard him say. 'I'm in a hurry here.'

'Jim,' said another voice, recognizing the driver, 'good to see you. Don't worry, it's just routine. The boss reckons there's a group of fugitives been hanging around town and he's asked us to check all vehicles.'

'Lawdy,' said Jim. Zoya heard him drop from the wagon onto the dust road. 'Well, I can assure you there ain't any stowaways in my wagon. You know me, the law's golden.'

'I know that, course I do. But it's the boss's orders.'

'So my word's not good enough for the army boys any more, eh?'

'It is. But rules is rules.'

Zoya heard Jimbo grumble under his breath, and felt the wagon kick as he climbed back into the driver's seat. Outside, the Aviation Army soldier bustled somewhere near the side of the wagon. By peeking through a small fold, Zoya was able to see a wedge of the road. In the distance, Deeplake stood lonely against the cliff, and to her left she could see the burgundy uniform of the soldier, jotting something onto a piece of paper.

She felt someone shift behind her. 'What can you see?' whispered Bucker.

'Shh.'

The soldier finished making his notes, and looked at his watch. He blinked to make sure he was reading it correctly, then rubbed his eyes. 'He's coming,' whispered Zoya.

Zoya reached down to grip her dagger. The man was close, pulling on a pair of leather gloves.

'Will you get on with it?' yelled Jim from the driver's seat.

'Won't be long.'

The soldier laid his hand on the blanket and tugged it slightly, dragging it over Zoya's hair. Then he checked his watch again, and a look of irritation crossed his face. He let go of the blanket and removed his gloves. 'I'm not paid enough for this,' he muttered. 'It's OK Jim, we don't need to do this. I trust you.' His footsteps crunched to the front of the wagon. 'But you've got to tell me if you see any sign of them, you hear?'

'If I see them,' said Jim, 'I'll bring them here myself!'

'You're a good man,' said the soldier. 'Go on then. Have a safe trip.'

'Yeah, yeah,' Jim muttered as he gunned the wagon's engine and pulled away. Beneath the blanket, they waited for the vehicle to roll along for a couple of minutes before releasing their breaths. Zoya let go of her dagger.

'Next time we need to escape anywhere,' she said, adjusting the blanket and closing her eyes, 'we fly!'

25

Much as they'd like to have ridden the wagon all the way to Dalmacia, other checkpoints would have sprouted sooner or later. Eva had them wait until the village was long behind them, then, one-by-one, they tumbled out the back of the wagon and onto the road. Zoya jumped first, landing with a jolt, then scudding across the road and ducking behind a bush. Bucker followed, then Dodsley and Eva. The wagon had travelled a hundred yards or so between Zoya and Eva, so they had to walk to meet up.

'Well, here we are,' said Bucker. 'Everyone OK?'

Dodsley showed his arm, which had a scrape. 'Though I'm pretty sure that was Eva's sword,' he joked.

'Where do we go now then?' Zoya aimed the question at Eva.

The road stretched ahead, Jim's wagon already a matchbox against the vista. Low, sandy hills rolled for a few miles, giving way to the monorail station—a tall, metallic building, out of which stretched the two rails Zoya had seen from the cliff. She could see the cabins clearly now——huge, green oblongs, bigger than the *Dragonfly*. Beyond, shimmering in the heat, soared the walls of Dalmacia, so high they masked the sky. The land rose as it approached the wall, so those on the monorail trains had the curious sensation of rising and yet never leaving the ground. Meandering up to the main city gates was the same dust road on which Zoya and the others were walking. Dotted along this were checkpoints, more substantial than the one they'd passed earlier, with guard towers and search lanterns. Queuing outside these were lines of people, snaking down the road.

'The best way in is the monorail,' said Eva. 'If we're lucky, they won't check our papers at the station. Can you see the entrance?'

Eva pointed to a smaller set of doors above the main gates, into which ran the two monorail cables. 'It goes straight into the city?' asked Zoya.

'Right into the middle.'

'Have you never been to Dalmacia?' asked Dodsley.

Zoya shook her head. 'Just to the museum. Not actually inside the city.'

Dodsley smiled. 'Oh boy, are you in for a treat.'

Zoya glanced at Eva. 'He's right,' she said. 'It's an amazing place. But we've got to get there first. We're about a two-day hike to the station. And if the Aviation Army's still chasing us and Kane's still out there, it probably won't be easy. I suggest we stay here for now, then travel when it's dark. We don't want to be seen from the air.'

'What about everyone, though?' said Bucker. 'We need to rescue them before Kane does something.'

'We're not going to be able to rescue them if we get caught ourselves,' said Eva.

Everybody looked to Zoya for a final decision. Zoya went red. She didn't know what to do any more than anyone else. If they moved, they might get caught. If they stayed, Kane might do something to her friends. There was risk if she moved, risk if she stayed.

'Zoya,' said Eva, her eyes fierce, 'trust me.'

Zoya trusted Bucker implicitly, and she was starting to trust Dodsley too. But there was something about Eva—a belief. This was Eva's territory. She knew what she was doing. 'We stay,' said Zoya.

Eva led them to the side of the road, where they set up camp behind a clump of brownish-grey bushes, hazy under the intense sun. Before leaving town, Eva had prepared some oatcakes and cheese chunks, as well as some nuts and berries. Bucker got these out of his knapsack. As they ate, Dodsley did most of the talking, telling them about his daring raids and favourite heists. Eva shared a few tales too, mainly from her time as an airship pilot, and Zoya and Bucker told about their favourite airship robberies.

After a while, the conversation died and Zoya lay on the ground, staring up at the clouds. Back on the *Dragonfly*, she'd spent most of her lookout shifts trying to recognize animals in the clouds, or faces, or shapes. She did this now as the burning sun arced across the sky and dipped to the horizon, blue-grey clouds rolling across a pink and orange canvas. Momentarily, Zoya thought she spotted the wispy shape of a locket, and it made her reach for her own. So many times she'd considered getting rid of the pendant, getting rid of her troubles. No longer. There was a determination about her now. Kane was scary, but she'd ended him once and she'd do it again.

Later, Zoya was roused by a hand on her shoulder. Above her loomed Eva, gear strapped to her back. 'It's time.'

Eva led them off not long after, cross-country, each taking a turn at the rear of the group to keep watch behind them. It was cold now the sun had dropped, but Zoya soon started to warm as she walked. Eva's route took them up hills, down hills, along the outskirts of small villages, beside railway tracks, criss-crossing shallow streams. Zoya watched her. She appeared to be using the stars as her guide, ignoring the looming beacon that was the Dalmacia wall, its crenels lit by thousands of pinprick lanterns. Every so often, they heard the rumble of a wagon back on the road and rushed to duck behind the nearest bush. They also heard the gentle whoosh of airships flying overhead, their figureheads catching the soft moonlight. Zoya followed the craft, wondering whether each was Aviation Army or Kane's men. Such thoughts made her feel exposed, and she drew closer to the group.

The night's walk drew to a close when the sun started to rise. Eva found them another shelter—this time a small cave on the lee side of a hill—where they dumped their packs and slumped to the floor. Once they'd rested a few minutes, Dodsley dragged himself to his feet and made a fire out of nearby leaves and sticks. It was small, barely reaching Zoya's knees at its highest, but it would have to do. They sat around the fire in silence, watching its dancing flames, before slowly, one-by-one, they slid off to sleep.

26

Zoya slept through the entire morning and most of the afternoon. When she woke, the sun was still high in the sky, though off to the west. She glanced back at the others, who were still sleeping. She considered rousing them, but decided against the idea. They needed as much sleep as they could get, especially Bucker. Instead, she rooted around in the mouth of the cave for more sticks and restarted the fire. Once she got it burning, she looked around to see what food remained. Eva had suggested they resupply at the monorail station, so there wasn't a great deal. But there was enough bacon and bread to rustle up some kind of breakfast, so she set the meat on a stick and toasted the bread.

Soon, the bacon started to sizzle and throw off a scent that woke the others up. 'Oh, thanks Zoya,' said Eva, smiling drowsily.

'No problem,' said Zoya. She served bacon onto slices of bread and handed one to each of them. 'It's the least I could do.'

They ate in silence. When they'd finished, Zoya beat down the fire and scattered it as best she could, just in case they were being followed.

'We made good ground yesterday,' said Eva, 'but we're still a couple of days' walk from the station.'

'Really?' said Bucker. He looked up at the city wall through the cave's entrance.

'That's the Dalmacian desert for you, always making people think things are in reach.'

'So what do we do?' said Zoya.

'Keep walking,' said Eva, pulling her backpack. 'It's all we can do.'

Eva led them out of the cave and along a narrow, winding path that rolled out across the desert. Living on an airship, Zoya was used to climbing netting and masts. Climbing the sandy rock was something new, and she felt her thighs and calves start to burn almost as soon as they set foot on the ground. She glanced at Bucker, whose face registered the same.

'There aren't many more of these hills, are there?' she asked Eva.

'I don't know,' said Eva. 'I've never been this way before. I'm normally in a wagon.'

Bucker pulled a face at Zoya, then walked on.

It grew colder as the night progressed, and Zoya pulled the jacket Eva had lent her out of her pack and slung it over her shoulders. The cold reminded her of the time she, Vaspine, and Beebee had climbed the mountain on the Island in the Sky to reach her father's vault. It seemed a lifetime ago.

After an hour, they began to draw close to the rock's summit. In spite of the danger, Zoya secretly wished it was daytime so she could look back across the land to Deeplake and the waterfall.

'You'll see the view some day,' said Dodsley, approaching her from behind. 'When all this is over.'

Zoya glanced up at Dodsley and smiled. Before she could respond, she heard a shout from somewhere in the darkness ahead. It was Bucker, and there was an edge to his voice that made her reach for her dagger. 'What is it?'

'Um . . .' Bucker paused as the wind whistled by. 'I don't really know. I think you'd better come and have a look.'

They found him behind a large bush. 'This better not be a joke . . .' said Zoya, but she trailed off. On the other side of the hill was a sight unlike any she'd seen. She blinked a couple of times, then squinted. 'Is everyone else seeing this?'

'I am,' said Dodsley.

Stretched across the valley below was an enormous, metal, mechanical man—longer than three airships, and two across. It lay on its back, one arm wedged behind its head and the other resting on its chest. Its left leg was on the ground, while the right was bent at the knee. Surrounding the creature were hundreds of oil lanterns, each throwing a cone of light across the body, creating a magical, halo effect. The figure must have been there a long time, for creeping over its body were large beds of moss, and growing out of the cracks between its armour plates were small, spindly trees. Zoya stared at the mechanoid from the top of the hill, unable to believe its size.

'I really, *really* want to go down,' said Bucker.

'Well, you're in luck,' said Eva. 'We have to.'

'What is it?' asked Zoya.

'I'd forgotten it was here, actually,' said Eva. 'It's a Titan.'

Zoya rolled the word around her tongue. 'Titan.'

Eva nodded. 'You've never heard of them?'

'They're not from around here, remember?' said Dodsley.

'I know, but I thought everybody knew about the Titans.'

'What are they?' said Zoya.

'That's the thing,' said Eva. 'No-one really knows.' She dropped down on a nearby rock and lowered her pack to the sand. 'There are twelve in total, spread across the world. They've been found in all sorts of places—up mountains, at the bottom of oceans, beneath deserts. This one was found by an archaeologist a hundred years ago.'

'Any theories?'

Eva shrugged. 'Lots. No-one's got anything definite, though.'

'We know they were alive,' said Dodsley. 'Or as alive as

a mechanical man can be. But who made them, and what they're for, no-one really knows.'

'Wow!' said Bucker. 'Just, wow!'

Eva smiled. 'I think they started giving people tours inside the Titan's head, but you're going to have to wait. We need to go down there, though, grab some food from one of those cabins.' She pointed to a collection of shacks near the Titan's feet. 'Then we need to get over the thing and on our way.'

Bucker frowned, but Zoya touched his arm to calm him. 'OK, OK,' he said, shaking her off. 'But when we're done with everything, we're coming back and I'm going inside.'

'I'll tell you what,' said Dodsley, 'if we're still alive, I'll come with you!'

27

Zoya thought about the Titan as they descended the hill. How could something so big have escaped detection until a hundred years ago? Perhaps it had been deposited there by someone around that time, disguised to look ancient? But if so, why? And if not, had the Titan been there long enough for the world to grow over it? How long might that take? A thousand years? Two? Zoya knew the world was old. Dalmacia had been around for a millennium, and the other big metropolises—Tamertin, Regnian, Zidesse, and Odessa—weren't much younger. But these were cities, constructed over ages. What if the Titans predated them all? The thought made her shiver.

Bucker was simply amazed. He led them swiftly to the bottom of the hill, to a point where the Titan lay directly ahead. Even though it was late, the area around the figure was busy, with people sipping drinks or eating food at picnic tables. Concerned they'd be recognized, Zoya surveyed the valley for another route.

'Going over the Titan's the quickest way,' said Eva, reading her mind. She tapped Bucker's shoulder. 'Pass me your knapsack.'

Bucker unhooked the bag from his shoulders and handed it to Eva. 'You can walk on them?' he asked.

'Of course,' said Eva, as though it were obvious.

'Brilliant!' said Bucker.

Eva smiled. 'Listen, I'm going to get us some food. Zoya, come with me. You two go and grab that picnic bench. If anyone talks to you, be friendly. We're just a normal group of people here to see the Titan.'

Zoya scoffed. 'I don't know about normal.' She followed Eva to the store—a small, wooden hut. As they neared the shack, Zoya caught the scent of toasted bread and meat, and felt her stomach rumble. They needed to get supplies, but Zoya intended to buy something hot as well, something to melt on her tongue. The owner of the hut was a short man with black hair and a mole on the end of his nose that matched another on his forehead. Looped around his neck was a black apron. As Eva and Zoya arrived, he finished wiping his hands on a towel. 'What can I do for you?'

Eva smiled. 'We're just passing through on our way to Dalmacia. We need some food to keep us going.'

'Say no more,' said the man. 'Bacon, biscuits, and cheese sound about right?'

'Perfect,' said Eva. 'Have you got any nuts?'

'Peanuts?'

'They'll do.'

'And I'll have one of the pork buns,' said Zoya. She grinned at Eva.

As the man prepared the food and placed it into Bucker's bag, he asked Eva where they were from, whether they'd seen the Titan before, what they thought of it. The conversation drifted over Zoya's head; she was so captivated by the sizzling meat. She stared at it like it was the first food she'd seen in weeks. She imagined the sandwich she was about to eat—crusty bun, pork, cheese, lettuce.

Zoya froze.

Tacked to the wall behind the cook was a piece of paper, upon which was scratched the Aviation Army logo. Printed beneath this in bold letters was the word 'Wanted' and beneath that the word 'Fugitives'. Further down, near the bottom of the poster, was a reasonably accurate sketch of her, Bucker, and Dodsley. The hairs on the back of Zoya's neck stood up. She felt an urge to run, to grab Eva's arm, drag her away and keep walking until the Titan was just a spot in the distance. But she knew that was the most suspicious thing she could do. Instead, she turned her face from the cabin as innocently as she could and tapped her foot on the floor, waiting for Eva to finish.

'That'll be five coins,' said the man.

As Eva grabbed the coins from her money pouch, Zoya

spotted Dodsley leave the picnic bench and walk towards them. She tried to catch his attention by glowering at him, but it was no good. When Dodsley reached the counter, he slid in behind Eva, slotted his arm through hers and started to pull her gently away. Eva, still fumbling in her purse, shrugged him off.

'There you are,' he said, trying again. 'You know, we'd better rush if we're going to see the Titan.' He sounded like any other tourist.

'I haven't paid for the food.' She smiled awkwardly at the chef.

'I know,' said Dodsley. 'But we don't want to miss anything.'

There was something strange about Dodsley's insistence. Zoya glanced at Bucker, still at the picnic table. When he saw Zoya, he gestured over her shoulder towards the Titan's feet. Zoya followed his gaze and understood immediately what was wrong. Off at the edge of the field, a transporter had just touched down, its lanterns drawing a neat circle on the ground. An eagle symbol identified it as Aviation Army. Two burly soldiers stepped out and brushed down their uniforms. 'I agree with Dodsley,' said Zoya, faking a sweet smile. 'I really think we should go. Our friends are here.'

This time, Eva read the message in Zoya's eyes and glanced behind her at the soldiers, who were now heading towards the picnic area. 'OK,' she said, regaining her composure and returning to the chef. 'I'm really sorry, but it looks like we're going to have to leave the food. You can guarantee I'll be back, though; that pork smells amazing!'

Eva smiled, but the chef knew something was wrong. He peered at her from behind the counter, then at Zoya and Dodsley. When his eyes locked onto Dodsley, a spark of recognition flashed across his face and he quickly turned to the 'Wanted' poster.

'Come on,' said Zoya, tugging at Eva's arm, 'we need to run.'

As they started to jog they heard the voice of the chef behind them. 'Hang on a minute,' he said, 'hang on! That's the guy from the poster. Quick, someone get him!'

Zoya, Dodsley, and Eva started to sprint towards Bucker. As they moved, Zoya glared at the other customers to ward them off making a move. Scaring off the Aviation Army wouldn't be as easy, and a quick glance told her they were aware of the commotion. Zoya arrived at Bucker's table just as the soldiers arrived at the food hut. She watched the chef lean down and point in their direction.

'Bucker,' said Dodsley. 'We're leaving.'

Bucker sprang to his feet and they crossed the picnic area, bounded up a set of metal stairs and vaulted over a barrier onto the stomach of the Titan. Their landing made enough noise to alert anyone who hadn't already spotted their escape. The picnickers on the ground were silent now, their eyes trained on the Titan. The Aviation Army soldiers drew their guns as they wound through the tables towards the staircase. Eva spoke quietly. 'Get the lights.'

'What?' Bucker looked at Zoya.

'Do it!' snapped Eva. 'We're not going to be able to escape this by running. Kill them.'

They moved swiftly across the Titan, smashing every lantern they encountered. Within thirty seconds, their section of the creature was dark, lit only by the crescent moon. Zoya could barely see anything. From her left, she heard Eva whisper. 'Dodsley?'

Silence. Then an almost imperceptible patter of footsteps. 'Yes?'

'I want you to take them out.'

Another pause. 'OK.'

Eva led Zoya and Bucker to an elevated section of armour plating, where they dropped to their hands and knees. The metal was gritty, cold. Zoya positioned herself so she could see around the plate. Somewhere in the darkness, Dodsley waited. She'd seen what he could do on the cliff-face with the two muggers, but those men had carried knives. The Aviation Army soldiers had guns. All they had to do was listen for a noise and fire in Dodsley's direction. Zoya spotted the soldiers' silhouettes, vaulting the railing and landing on the Titan. She watched them edge towards the centre of the creature, then lost them in the darkness. Suddenly, there was a flurry of movement, a rustling and scratching. This continued for a few seconds, before she heard a low grunt. Dodsley's silhouette rose into the light, then instantly, a *rat-a-tat* of gunfire cut the silence. Dodsley dived back into the shadows.

From within the darkness came a gruff voice. 'You got the rookie, son. You won't get me.'

Everything returned to silence. Zoya peered into the black, desperate for her eyes to adjust. She was starting to pick out shapes now—raised areas on the Titan's chest, the outlines of smashed lanterns. Zoya longed to rush out and help Dodsley, but she knew she'd as likely run into the soldier.

Instead, she watched.

After a few seconds, a shape loomed large ahead. Zoya could tell by the sweep of the figure's shoulders that it was the soldier. She watched him stalk forwards, his gun poised, his left hand feeling for obstacles. She expected Dodsley to swoop down on him, a blur of arms and legs. Instead, she spotted the thief to her left, peering into the gloom, one hand stretched ahead and the other gripping a nearby armour plate. The soldier spotted Dodsley at the same time as Zoya did. He froze, waited a few seconds, then started to move forwards.

Zoya covered her mouth to stop from shouting Dodsley's name and giving away their position. But she had to do something. A panic swept over her and she felt like crying, but she forced herself out from behind the armour plate and sprinted across the Titan's belly towards the soldier, each footstep ringing on the metal. Both the soldier and Dodsley snapped their heads at the sound, but it was too late for the soldier. Zoya barrelled into his stomach at full speed, sending them both sprawling to the metal. They rolled together for a few yards—rivets smashing into Zoya's back—before coming to a stop near the Titan's ribs. Zoya was pinned under the soldier, his entire bulk pressing down through his knee onto her right arm. She screamed in pain, and a cold smirk snaked across his lips. Holding her in place, he groped across the metal for his gun and aimed its barrel at Zoya's face. 'Trying to take me out, eh? You don't stand a chance.'

'No,' said Dodsley, to their left, 'but I do.' He swung a length of metal around his head and connected solidly with the back of the soldier's. The soldier remained still for a moment, then slumped down to the metal.

Dodsley helped Zoya up. 'You shouldn't have done that,' he said. 'These men are trained to kill.'

'That's what friends do,' she said.

Dodsley smiled, then hugged Zoya. 'Come on, I think we need to get away from this thing. It's more dangerous than it looks.'

28

They jogged for the next two hours, trying to put as much desert sand as they could between themselves and the Titan. Only when Eva was satisfied they'd left the Titan far enough behind did she allow them to walk.

'You tired?' asked Dodsley, looking down at the kids.

Zoya shook her head. 'Those . . .' she hesitated, '. . . those soldiers, they hadn't done anything wrong. They were just doing their job.'

'Oh, they've got plenty of dirt on their hands,' said Dodsley. He exchanged a glance with Eva.

Zoya shook her head.

Sensing the tension, Bucker changed the subject. 'How much longer until we get to the monorail?' he asked.

Eva peered into the darkness. 'We're nearly there,' she said. 'A few more miles. We can stop here for the night. When we wake up, we'll walk the last bit.'

Bucker breathed a sigh of relief, took off his backpack

and dropped it to the ground. He joined the bag, flopping backwards so that he lay flat. 'Well,' he said, grinning, 'all this watching other people fight has worn me out. I'm beat!'

Zoya smiled. 'Eva, do you want me to get some firewood?'

'That'd be good.' Eva slumped down next to Bucker and reclined on her elbows. For the first time since Deeplake, she looked tired.

'C'mon,' Zoya said to Dodsley, 'we'll sort everything tonight. I think these two need a rest. Who's got the food?'

'We haven't got any,' said Eva.

'Let's do the fire then.' Zoya shrugged.

Zoya and Dodsley left the others on the ground. Either side of the road were vast stretches of land, unbroken except for the odd hill. Trees were rare in the desert, and they had to walk half a mile before they came across anything substantial. A tall, bare tree stood out in the open, next to a winding stream. Zoya and Dodsley gathered broken branches from beneath the tree, and when these weren't enough, tore a few from above. As they worked, Zoya asked Dodsley a question. 'It was something to do with the Aviation Army, wasn't it?'

'What?'

'You and Eva.'

Dodsley rubbed the bruise on his forehead where Eva had hit him a couple of days before. 'Something like that.'

Zoya put down her branches and turned to Dodsley. 'What did you do?'

Dodsley arched his eyebrows. 'What did I do?'

'Well, she's the one who wants to kill *you*.'

Dodsley placed down his sticks and sat on one of the tree's roots. 'Listen, those stories are never as one-sided as people make them sound.'

'What happened then?'

Dodsley sighed. 'Eva and I met in the back of an Aviation Army wagon. Did she tell you that?'

Zoya nodded.

'After that, we were inseparable.'

'Aww.' Zoya giggled.

'Yeah,' said Dodsley, 'it was like that for a bit.'

She waited for more.

'Did she tell you about the Constaff robbery?'

Zoya shook her head.

'It was big; our biggest yet——a commission from the richest criminal in Dalmacia, Christopher Ellesworth. His niece was a musician and he wanted me to steal an antique violin from the Constaff concert hall. Do you know it?'

Zoya thought about it. 'Nope.'

'You'll have seen it if you've flown over Dalmacia in the air. It's the tall building that sticks up above the rest.'

Zoya nodded.

'We got the violin pretty easily——in and out through the roof.' Dodsley snapped his fingers. 'For an escape route, we'd strung a wire from the Constaff all the way down to an alley half a mile away. We were climbing down it, me first, Eva behind. When we got near the bottom I heard Eva cry out. She'd got herself snagged on the wire.'

'Hmm,' said Zoya.

'Yeah, well get this: I start to make my way back up to free her, when suddenly an Aviation Army transporter blazes over the rooftop.'

Zoya cringed. 'Please tell me you didn't run.'

'What choice did I have? If I stayed, we'd both get caught. That way, not only do we both end up in prison, but we have Christopher Ellesworth on our cases.'

'Please tell me you didn't leave her hanging there.'

'I had to!' said Dodsley. 'There was no point both of us going to prison. At least if one of us got away, we might be able to get the other out.'

'So what did you do?'

Dodsley winced. 'I looked at the transporter, then her. She knew what I was going to do before I did it.' He paused. 'I got myself out of there.'

Zoya shook her head.

Dodsley took a breath, then pushed himself off the root, picked up his branches and reached back up to the tree. 'Easy in hindsight. Not so easy when you're making the choice.'

'So that's why she hates you?'

'She doesn't hate me,' said Dodsley. 'She just hasn't forgiven me yet.'

Zoya sat in silence, considering what he'd said, then picked up her own pile and started to search for more. 'Did you at least try to rescue her?' she asked.

'Of course,' said Dodsley. 'Of course I did. I managed to get to her cell window that night with some cutters. But . . .'

'But what?'

'She wouldn't come.'

Zoya stared.

'It's true. She just looked at me, told me if I came any nearer she'd kill me, then turned away and sat back in her cell.'

'So, you rescued her and she wouldn't come?'

Dodsley nodded.

'Wow,' said Zoya. 'She must have been seriously annoyed.'

'After that, we didn't speak to each other until she smashed me over the head in Deeplake.'

Zoya whistled through her teeth. They finished collecting wood in silence, then located the camp in the distance and started to walk. 'She doesn't really hate you,' said Zoya. 'I can tell.'

'I know,' said Dodsley, reaching up to rub his bruise again. 'She's just got a funny way of showing it.'

29

They found Eva and Bucker back at the camp. 'This is going to be visible from the air, isn't it?' said Zoya, setting up the fire.

'Yeah,' said Eva. 'It's not so bad on this stretch, though. People walk along here to the monorail station, so there are always a few fires.'

As the fire grew warm, Eva and Bucker dragged themselves up from the sand and joined Zoya and Dodsley nearby, their legs tucked up to their chins. In front of the fire, their chests grew warm while their backs remained cold. The fire reminded Zoya of happy bonfires back at the orphanage, when they'd burn all the broken chairs and tables from the previous year, and eat baked potatoes, and apples dunked in caramel. She watched goggle-eyed as the fire threw out sparks and cinders like a miniature firework display. Then Zoya noticed something strange. One spark seemed to hang in the air, even after a gust of wind had shifted the others.

She stared at it through tired eyes, then realized it wasn't a spark from the fire, but a distant light in the sky.

'What's that?' she asked, sitting up abruptly. Her movement caused the others to take notice, and they followed the line of her gaze until they located the light. As soon as Eva spotted it, she lay back down and closed her eyes.

'It's an airship,' she said.

Bucker frowned. 'Seems bright for an airship?'

'Yeah,' said Zoya. She stood to get a better view.

'I agree,' said Dodsley. 'Something's not right about that, Eva.'

Zoya and Bucker gathered their belongings, then joined Eva and Dodsley under a bush. They lay in silence, their breathing raspy against the cold night air. The craft— whatever it was—drifted towards them over the course of a few minutes, until it was less than a mile away. Even at that distance, Zoya could tell the vessel was on fire. As it approached, shapes started to reveal themselves within the flames, growing clearer by the minute, until Zoya realized that only specific sections of the hull were alight. The flames stretched across the ship horizontally, from deck to keel.

'What is it?' whispered Bucker.

'I think it spells something,' said Eva.

Zoya had never considered the shapes could be letters, but now Eva mentioned it she started to pick out letters in every line and curve. Only simple characters at first—here

171

an 'E' there a 'T'. But as the craft floated closer, a phrase started to emerge; one written in flames across its hull. It was a message, Zoya realized. A horrible, horrible message.

I see you, Zoya DeLarose. You cannot escape.
Come to me in two days, or your friends die.

Hidden beneath the bush, no-one spoke. The airship drifted over their heads and on towards the Dalmacia wall. When it had travelled far enough to once again become an orange blob, first Bucker and then the others pulled themselves out onto the sand. Zoya came last, her eyes fixed on the burning shape in the sky, a single tear on her left cheek. Eva put an arm around her. 'We're going to save them,' she said, turning Zoya's face and staring into her eyes. 'We'll get them.'

Zoya stared at her blankly. 'Which way's Dalmacia?'

Eva nodded over her shoulder. Zoya started to walk in the direction she'd suggested. Bucker jogged after her, leaving Dodsley and Eva a few yards behind. 'Looks like we're off,' said Dodsley.

Eva glanced again at the burning airship, a tiny red dot now, then up at the Dalmacia wall, cream in the glow of a thousand lanterns. 'I think it's going to be tougher than we thought,' she said.

30

They started to pass signs for the monorail station an hour or so after sunrise. The signs were isolated at first, but more frequent as tributary roads joined the main one. Traffic also joined them as they approached the station—wagons, cars, people walking—until they were part of a long line of travellers all heading in one direction.

Bucker was the first to spot the station as it crept over the horizon. It was an arresting building, perched on top of a gentle desert-rise like a mountain fort, with the sun illuminating it from behind. Shaped like a castle, with a crenellated roofline and a tower at each corner, the station was constructed from the same stone blocks as the city wall—vast, sandy slabs larger than a transporter. The station had two storeys, the lower receiving carriages from Dalmacia and the upper sending them back. Along either side of the road that led to the station were dozens of market stalls, each meeting the needs of weary travellers. Zoya ran up to one of these and fumbled in her pocket for change. 'Four pastries, please.'

The woman behind the counter took in her grubby clothes and face. She arched her eyebrows, then served up the food. 'You enjoy those.'

Zoya paid for the pastries and took one for herself. The others received theirs gratefully, before shovelling them into their mouths. 'I'm assuming we've still got money for the tickets,' said Zoya, between chomps.

'Plenty,' said Eva.

Once they'd finished their pastries, Eva led them to the ticket booth—a small, white hut. It was still early morning, so there was no queue. Eva put out a hand, signalling for the others to hang back, then strode up to the window. 'We'd like . . .' she turned to count, '. . . four tickets to Dalmacia, please.'

A queasy feeling in her stomach told Zoya something was about to go wrong, that Aviation Army soldiers were about to leap out from behind a nearby wall. But they didn't. Instead, the teller merely glanced at them to check Eva's number, smiled, then ripped four tickets off a blue roll. He punched each one, then handed them to Eva. She placed money for the fares on the counter.

'You're in luck today,' said the teller, taking the money and depositing it in a metal tin. 'There've been some problems with the rails. They've had to close down a few of the stops, so it should be a quick journey.'

'Brilliant,' said Eva. 'Thanks.'

Eva placed the tickets carefully in her pouch, then gestured for the others to follow her through the gate and into the station. After spending two nights on the plains with just the cliff, the sky, and the Dalmacia wall for company, Zoya felt a little overwhelmed by the bustle inside. They'd emerged into the main atrium, a bright room into which light streamed through huge windows, and an open wall at the opposite end. The opening—through which carriages entered the station—was quite a sight. Zoya jogged up to take a look. The view ran for miles, covering a vast expanse of rolling land dotted with villages, rising all the way to the city. She traced two thick rails back from the wall into the station. Running alongside the rails in the station were yet more cafés, taverns, food shops, and bookstores. And beyond these, two wide staircases.

'Wow,' said Bucker. 'You can see the wall of Dalmacia.'

'I know,' said Zoya. 'Now we just need to get up there.'

Eva and Dodsley joined them. 'Is anyone still hungry?' asked Eva.

Zoya shook her head.

'Buck?'

'I could eat something,' said Bucker. Dodsley also nodded.

'In which case, why don't you two grab some food and meet us by the platform upstairs,' said Eva.

Dodsley nodded at Bucker, then together they marched

off towards the nearest café. Eva held out a hand for Zoya, who took it. 'How are you holding up?' she asked, as they ascended the stairs to the second level.

'I'm OK.' Zoya shrugged. 'I'm a bit worried about Bucker. He hasn't mentioned his mum since the crash.'

Eva shrugged. 'We all handle things differently. And besides, didn't you say he'd been a sky thief longer than you?'

'Pretty much his whole life,' said Zoya.

'He's probably used to it then. He seems OK to me. You, on the other hand . . .'

'I'm fine,' said Zoya.

The station's second floor was much quieter than the first, with just a handful of people waiting patiently on benches for the announcement of the first train to Dalmacia. Zoya walked past them to the end of the building and found a metal railing on which to perch. To her left, the opening in the wall led out towards Dalmacia. Eva slumped down next to her and stared up at the city. After a while, Eva reached her hands around the back of her neck and unclipped her necklace. She enclosed it in her right hand and held it out to Zoya. Zoya stared at the hand quizzically.

'Go on,' said Eva. 'I saw you looking at it back at the house.'

'What, take it?' asked Zoya.

'Yes, go on.'

'I can't. It's yours.'

Eva laughed. 'I always wanted a little sister to give my jewellery. You can be the one I never had.'

Zoya rolled her eyes, smiled, and took the pendant from Eva's hand. 'Thank you.' She hooked the pendant around her neck and let it hang next to her own. 'Does it look nice?'

Eva nodded. 'Beautiful. They go together.' A few seconds of silence passed as Zoya twirled her new necklace. Then Eva nodded at the city in the distance. 'I used to live there, you know?'

'I know,' said Zoya.

'It's dangerous. I was scared every day we'd be caught by the army.'

'You were caught.'

Eva chuckled. 'He told you.'

Zoya nodded.

'I bet he told you about him coming to rescue me too?'

Zoya nodded again.

'I knew he'd come,' said Eva. 'Even though he'd left me on the wire, I knew he'd come.'

'Why didn't you go with him then?' asked Zoya.

Eva shrugged. 'Pride? I don't know. That's not the point. The point is I knew he'd come. Because that's what people do when their friends are in trouble.'

'I get what you're saying. You think they're waiting for us.' Zoya turned to face Eva. 'But they may not have that chance. You don't know Kane.'

'No,' said Eva, 'but I'm getting to know you. And if your friends are half as brave as you are, they'll be fighting to stay alive because they know you're coming.'

Nearby, one of the waiting carriage's engines burst to life, causing the cabin to judder and vibrate. A conductor down the platform heard the noise. He straightened his uniform before starting to make his way down the passageway, inviting those waiting to step on board.

'So, what if you're right?' said Zoya. 'What if they are alive? We still don't know where they are, or how we're going to get them.'

Eva smiled. 'You leave finding out Kane's location to me. I might have been in hiding for a while, but it takes more than a few years digging rocks to make me forget my tricks.' She pushed herself off the railing and brushed down her trousers. 'Now, let's get ourselves a seat before the boys get here and steal the good ones.'

31

Presently, Bucker and Dodsley joined them, their arms filled with more pastries, oatcakes, slices of ham and cheese. Zoya was suddenly hungry. She grabbed another pastry and ate it as the carriage started to fill.

Zoya had never ridden a monorail before. It reminded her of the ground-based transporters that used to stop outside the orphanage. Its seats were arranged in split rows—two to a seat—each with its own window. The floor was polished wood with a shiny metal trim that—when combined with the velvet seat coverings—made Zoya feel like she was somewhere important. Standing behind an ornate counter at the front of the carriage was a woman selling food. In the corner, there to cater to the whim of the train's travellers, was the conductor.

Bucker turned to Zoya. 'This is pretty cool.'

'Yeah,' said Zoya, glancing out the window. 'Yeah, it is.'

The carriage left the station, jerking as it attached itself to the rail. It made a screeching noise as it pulled away, before slowly gaining speed. Zoya watched the station recede through her window as the train started its long journey, rising from the desert floor to the heights of Dalmacia.

For the next half an hour, Zoya sat with her forehead on the window, her eyes pressed up against the glass, staring at the city as its curved wall grew bigger and bigger. In time, the wall came to dominate Zoya's entire view, obscuring even the sky. She could see the cracks between individual blocks now, and if she strained to look down, the main gate for people arriving at the city on foot. Ahead, the tracks rose to the wall, before entering the city through a narrow gap surrounded by huge, wooden support beams. Buzzing about this were a dozen airships. Zoya peered closely to see if any were Aviation Army, but this time they were safe.

The carriage passed the last mile in silence, half its passengers with their faces buried in books or playing with bamboo puzzles. The others, for whom the monorail was a new experience, were conspicuous by their enchanted faces. Even Zoya and Bucker, who'd flown over the city countless times in the *Dragonfly*, held their breaths. From above, the city looked incredible. But entering on the monorail, with the entire metropolis spread out like the pages of a book, it was something else entirely.

When the carriage was only a few dozen yards away, the air-port doors slid open to reveal a city glinting in the sunlight.

Zoya cringed as the train slid through the narrow gap and into the city airspace. She drank in the view. The city was alive—a writhing mass of houses, parks, factories, smoke-stacks, oil refineries, roads, alleys, railway lines, cables, airships, transporters, and more. Built up, torn down, and built up again over the course of a thousand years, the city was a jungle. In the centre was the Constaff concert hall Dodsley had told Zoya about, and next to that the jewel-encrusted dome of the Imperial Palace.

The monorail's tracks cut across the sky, ducked under a connecting bridge, and began to descend into the heart of the city. As they sank, Zoya caught glimpses of Aviation Army regiments on manoeuvres, a steam train on the ground chugging towards the city wall, an old woman hanging washing on a balcony, a man watering crops on his rooftop, a team of labourers unloading rocks from the back of a wagon. 'This is incredible.'

Soon, the carriage had dropped into the shadows between the buildings, then further down until it was just a tree's height from the ground, where it disappeared into the waiting mouth of Dalmacia station. Inside, the craft ground to a halt, jolting as it did. Zoya, Bucker, Dodsley, and Eva stepped onto the platform.

Immediately, a smell hit Zoya—a grubby, oily, city smell. It hung thick in the air, making her gag. Eva must have seen this, for she burst out laughing. 'Don't worry,' she said to Zoya, 'you get used to it.'

They exited the station onto a narrow road, thronging with people. Lining the street were brightly lit storefronts—inns, pubs, grocers, blacksmiths, tailors, cobblers. Eva stood on the steps that led down from the station and took a breath. 'Feels like home,' she said. She faced the others. 'To find out where Kane's got your friends, we need to go deep into the city. Keep your wits about you.' She glanced at Zoya and Bucker. 'Not everyone here is friendly.'

Eva darted down the steps and took an immediate left, passing the shops. The others followed. Eva led them through the crowd, sliding by anyone moving slowly, or waiting patiently when she didn't have a choice. At the end of the street they came to a crossroads beside a huge cathedral, at least three times the size of the *Dragonfly*. The cathedral was surrounded by a ring of grass, where kids skipped or threw balls or relaxed in the sun. Zoya stared at the building, unable to believe something so massive could stand in the centre of the city and still be dwarfed by everything nearby. Next to the Constaff concert building and Imperial Palace, it seemed positively tiny.

Eva's route took them past the church and down a stone stairwell. This first staircase led into the depths of the city, and to Zoya it felt like they spent the next hour descending dark stairways, crossing busy streets, and creeping down even darker alleys. The houses and shops grew smaller as they went, and shabbier, with peeling paint, crumbling brickwork, toppled roof tiles, boarded-up windows, and flattened fences. Sitting on steps were beggars, their caps laid out in front. Zoya spotted the furtive, sideways glances of pickpockets on more than one occasion.

'It's not like that top bit down here, is it?' said Bucker.

'No,' said Eva, as she searched the street to find her way. 'Money doesn't trickle down in Dalmacia, it flows up.' She cast a glance at the Imperial Palace, still dominating the view in spite of their depth. Then they were off again—this time to the end of the street, through a gate and along a murky canal. They tracked the canal for a while—flashing their weapons at any mean-looking characters they encountered—until they came to another flight of stairs. They climbed these and emerged onto a wider road. Eva looked around, then glanced at Dodsley. He nodded.

'You sure?' she said.

'This is it,' said Dodsley. 'Mika's is just down there.'

Dodsley took the lead now, guiding the others down the street, sticking to the shadows, until they were hunched under the same archway as he had been a week or so before. 'There it is,' he said, nodding across the street. 'Who's going in?'

'I can do it myself,' said Eva.

'You haven't been there for a while,' said Dodsley.

Eva frowned. 'Well, we can't leave the kids out here alone.'

'They'll have to come in.'

Eva bit her lips, trying to think of another plan. 'OK,' she said. She turned to the kids. 'But you don't say a word, is that clear?'

Zoya and Bucker nodded.

Eva took a breath, then led them across the street and into the tavern. They used the entrance Dodsley had used before meeting Kane, sneaking to the alley and clambering over the wall. It was still morning, and the tavern was quieter than Dodsley's last visit. Aside from Mika, busy shining glasses behind the bar, there were only two others inside—a couple of old men in a corner booth nursing muddy-looking pints. Eva paused in the doorway to scope out the exits in case of an emergency, then walked up to the bar. Mika didn't recognize her at first, but after a moment a smile spread across his face. He placed the glass on the counter, made his way out from behind the bar and laid two big hands on Eva's shoulders. 'Are my eyes deceiving me?'

'Hi Mika.'

'But I thought the Aviation Army nabbed you?' said Mika. 'Last I heard, you were in jail.'

'I was,' said Eva. She winked.

Mika stared at her, impressed. 'Well,' he said, 'well, well. Where have you been? I haven't seen you in years!'

'I got out of it all,' said Eva. 'I've been living in Deeplake, mining up the cliff.'

Mika leaned back and inspected her. 'Little Eva, living the quiet life? That can't be right.'

'It is,' said Eva.

Mika laughed. 'What do you know? And who's this behind you?' Mika glanced at the others. When he recognized Dodsley, he nodded. 'I see you're still alive. For now.'

Dodsley nodded in return. 'By the skin of my teeth.'

'You're a lucky boy.' He turned to Zoya and Bucker. 'And who might be these two cherubs?'

'I'm Bucker,' said Bucker, 'and this is Zoya.'

Eva shot a glance at Bucker, who shut his mouth quickly.

'I see,' said Mika, understanding Eva's caution. 'Well, that will be yours and my little secret, won't it master?' He turned back to Eva. 'Why don't you and your friends grab a seat? I'll get my cook to bring you some breakfast.'

'Thanks, but we don't have time . . .'

'Nonsense,' said Mika, cutting her off. 'Grab a seat and I'll be right over.' Mika waddled off into the kitchen, as Eva shrugged and selected a table.

'We need his advice,' she said, catching Zoya's glare. 'Just be patient.'

Mika returned a few minutes later with four plates of eggs, bacon, sausages, beans, and toast. Zoya fell on the food like a dog. While they ate, Mika brought over a pot of coffee, which he poured into mugs and handed around. He poured his own last and took a sip.

'Now, old Mika ain't as sharp as he used to be, but something tells me you wouldn't have come here if you didn't have a problem.'

Eva nodded. 'I need information. But I don't want to get you in trouble.'

'You wouldn't be the first to bring it.'

'OK.' Eva took a breath. 'I need to know where Lendon Kane is.'

Mika shot a glance at Dodsley, then frowned. 'And why would you want to know that?'

'He has something of ours. We want it back.'

Mika sat back in his seat. 'I've known you since you were a little girl, Eva Hart. You've never been the type to risk your skin for sentimentality. There's more to this than you're letting on. You either tell me, or you walk out the door.'

Eva looked at Zoya, who nodded.

'Kane attacked Zoya and Bucker's ship two nights ago. He took their crew-mates. We're going to get them back.'

Mika blew a gust of air through his lips, then looked again at Dodsley. 'So, the job did bring trouble?'

'We can fix it,' said Dodsley.

'I'm sure you can. I'm also sure Kane could fix the lot of you, given the chance. It's too dangerous.' He turned to Bucker and Zoya. 'You kids shouldn't be playing with this. You're too young. Thank your lucky stars you got away and start again, get out of sky thieving for good.'

Zoya stood up. 'We were the ones who destroyed the *Shadow* last year,' she hissed, louder than intended. 'We've beaten Kane before and we'll do it again!'

'Is that right?' said Mika, looking to Eva and Dodsley for confirmation. They nodded. Mika laughed. 'Well well, who'd have thought it?'

Zoya sat down. 'Listen, sir, my friends are in trouble. I want to save them. If you don't want to help us we'll find someone who will.'

Mika was still laughing. 'All right, all right, I can see you're set.' He leaned in. 'Word has it he's taken the survivors to his fortress.'

'Where?' said Dodsley.

'The Island in the Sky. South of the island. But it's heavily defended.'

'We'll deal with that,' said Eva. 'We need a transporter to get up there.'

'A transporter?' repeated Mika. 'Are you sure they can even fly that high?'

'We'll find out,' said Eva.

'Well,' said Mika, 'I can't help you with that anyway.'

'We don't need you to get one for us,' said Eva. 'I'm owed money by one of my old bosses. I just need you to tell me where he is.'

'You sure you want to do that? You know how these people get when someone calls.'

'Trust me, we'll be fine.'

'Go on then, give me a name.'

'Knottingham.'

'Knottingham.' A crease appeared on Mika's forehead. 'Severn Knottingham?'

Eva nodded.

Mika gestured behind her. 'If you want Knottingham, you've come to the right place. He's right out back.'

32

Eva looked towards a doorway at the back of the tavern.

'Whatever you do,' said Mika, 'don't cause trouble. I've had enough of the Aviation Army around here recently.'

Eva didn't respond. Instead, she pushed herself up from her seat and started to walk to the door. Dodsley smiled awkwardly, nodded his head, then got up and motioned for the kids to follow. 'Be careful,' Dodsley said to Eva.

'It's him who needs to be careful.'

Eva slammed open the door, prompting a flurry of activity inside. Three big bearded men leapt to their feet, sending chairs flying against the wall and spilling drinks onto the floor. From their wrists, they each drew a knife that glinted in the light of the room's single oil lantern. Seated between them was Severn Knottingham. When he saw Eva, he laid his hand of cards slowly on the table. 'Most people who burst in on me like this don't leave with a full set of fingers,' he said, his voice calm.

'I could say the same about people who steal from me,' said Eva.

The others had managed to enter the room now. Dodsley moved to stand beside Eva. Severn stared at her, his face scrunched up in thought, before he gestured for his men to sit. 'Eva, I haven't seen you in five years. Sit down, take a drink.'

'I'd rather stand,' said Eva. 'I don't intend staying for long.'

Severn picked up a glass from the table, swallowed the brown liquid, then slapped it back down. He was a stout, squat man, with wrinkled skin that looked like it had been dragged beneath a wagon. His face was animal-like, with narrow, craggy slits for eyes and wide, sticking-out ears. On his head he wore a neat trilby hat, and from his left ear dangled a fish-shaped earring. In spite of his calm manner, there was an air of menace about him, a flash in his eye that told Zoya he'd as soon slice them up as talk.

'You know,' said Knottingham, glancing at them one by one, 'I've come to this tavern and sat in this room playing cards at the same time, every day, for the past ten years. In all that time, no-one has ever disrupted me like this. Do you know why?'

He aimed the question at Dodsley.

'It's because I'm Severn Knottingham,' he continued. 'I own this town. Tell your lady friend what that means, young man.'

The man to Severn's right jumped in before Dodsley could answer. 'It means you're either stupid, or you've got a death wish.'

'I want my money,' said Eva, stepping forward. Severn's men leaned in, causing her to stop. 'You owe me five hundred coins for the painting.'

Severn laughed. 'Ha! Is that it? That's all you want?' He shooed her away. 'It's an insult. Get out of here!'

'You're going to give me my money,' said Eva.

Severn rose from his seat like a cobra and moved swiftly around the table. He was in Eva's face in a second, liquor breath in her nostrils. 'Oh yeah? And what are you going to do about it?'

'I did what you asked,' said Eva, her voice calm. 'I went to the gallery. I stole the painting. I brought it to you. You never paid.'

'You failed to get it to me on time.'

'I was an hour late,' said Eva. 'And I offered to reduce my fee.'

'Late goods, no fee. That's always been my way.' Severn stepped away from Eva and towards Dodsley, leaning forward so that Dodsley had to lean back to avoid bumping into the older man's face.

'It's not my way,' said Eva. 'I want my money.'

Suddenly, Severn spun back to Eva, rearing on his toes and shoving her in the chest. 'You come here to my favourite

191

bar,' he roared, 'telling me you want my money.' He shoved her again. 'I'm going to take you and your little friends here and chop you into . . .'

Dodsley's fist landed square on Severn's chin, stopping him mid-sentence. The short man stared ahead, eyes wide, mouth open in the shape of the word he'd been about to say, then slumped slowly to the floor. He landed with his head on Dodsley's foot, snoring softly. It took a while for Severn's men to realize what had happened. When they did, they tossed the table aside and started to advance. 'Run!' shouted Eva.

Zoya led the escape, dodging between booths, past the bar and out the front door. She came to a standstill outside, unsure where to go. The others crashed into her from behind, sending them all tumbling to the ground. 'This way!' yelled Dodsley, as they picked themselves up.

He led them back down the street in the direction of the canal, flinging over rubbish bins and food carts to slow down their pursuers. They reached the canal with Severn's men still fifty yards behind, pumping their legs to catch up. Dodsley vaulted the gate and shoved it open from the other side so that Zoya, Bucker, and Eva could slip through. 'What now?' asked Zoya.

'This way.'

Dodsley led them down the canal, running as fast as he could towards a bridge in the distance. When they reached it, Dodsley sprinted beneath the arch and abruptly stopped.

He glanced down the path to make sure the men were still some way off. 'Give me a hand with this,' he said. He darted over to where the path met the canal, dropped to his stomach and groped around near the waterline. Zoya heard a small click, then Dodsley started to haul up a metal panel from the side of the canal. Zoya got on her belly and helped him lift. 'Quick, get inside!' said Dodsley.

First Bucker, then Eva and Zoya swung themselves over the edge of the canal and slotted their legs into the gap. It was tight inside, barely wide enough for them all to fit. Dodsley entered last, then quickly leaned out over the water and grabbed the cover from the path. This, he manoeuvred into position near their heads, then locked it into place. For thirty seconds they lay in the darkness, panting heavily, until they heard the sound of footsteps above. The steps came to a stop a few feet down the path, causing Zoya to cringe. Then she heard voices. 'Where did they go?'

'I don't know,' said another, this one's voice gruff. She heard the two men step around above the bridge, walking first one way, then the other.

'They're like ghosts.'

'No wonder she was such a good thief.'

There was a moment's silence.

'You know, I've had enough of this. Let's just tell the boss they ran into some Aviation Army lads and we had to pull back. Yeah?'

'Yeah. I ain't chasing them up and down here all day. C'mon.'

They listened in the darkness as the two men tramped back up the path. After a few seconds, Zoya nudged Dodsley to get out, but he resisted for a while to avoid any tricks. However, eventually, when still they'd heard nothing, Dodsley unlatched the panel, pushed it into the water and hauled himself onto the path. He checked to make sure the men had gone, then stretched down a hand to help the others. When they were free, Dodsley leaned over the edge, scooped up the panel from the water and slotted it back in place. 'I knew that would come in useful,' he said, brushing mud off his shirt.

'Why on earth do you have that?' asked Zoya.

'I get all my business from Mika's,' he said. 'I'd need five hands to count the times I've had to run from the place. I thought I'd tip the odds in my favour.'

'Nice,' said Bucker. 'Vaspine would like that.'

Zoya smiled. 'Yeah.'

'Sorry Eva,' said Dodsley, turning around. 'I couldn't help myself.'

'Don't worry,' said Eva. 'I was about to hit him too.'

They all laughed. 'What do we do now?' asked Bucker, when they'd finished. 'If we haven't got any money, we can't get a ship.'

Eva looked at Bucker like he'd lost his mind. 'What do they teach you sky thieves? Haven't you stolen anything?

If Severn's not going to give me the money, we'll steal his airship.'

Dodsley chuckled. This quickly turned into a laugh. Zoya and Bucker looked up at him, puzzled. Dodsley's eyes remained on Eva. 'This is what you wanted all along, wasn't it?'

'What do you mean?' asked Eva, innocently.

'You wanted to take his ship.'

'I don't know what you're talking about.' Eva flicked her head to hide a grin. 'Now, let's stop talking about what I did and didn't intend, and let's go.'

33

Eva led them along the canal, up the chain of staircases and back to the busy commercial streets.

'Where's the ship?' asked Dodsley as they walked.

'I'm assuming it's where it was before,' said Eva, 'in the northern air-dock. We can ride the elevator up, though I've no idea how we're going to steal it.'

'I was thinking about that,' said Zoya. 'We're going to have to get to the bridge. They're not just going to let us walk on.'

Dodsley grinned. 'Leave that bit to me. I've had an idea. I'll drop you off somewhere in a few minutes. Wait for me there.'

'How long are you going to be?' asked Eva.

'As long as it takes.'

Eva stared at him out of the corner of her eye, then shrugged. 'I guess you've helped them get this far. Maybe you're not as useless as I thought.'

'Is that an apology?'

Eva didn't respond. They turned a corner and Dodsley gestured to a statue of a lion, next to a blacksmiths. 'Wait there. Don't move.'

The others wandered up to the stone as Dodsley disappeared into the mass of people.

'I wonder if we'll see him again,' muttered Eva.

'We will,' said Zoya.

Time passed in a blur of people. City-living was so different to Zoya's normal, everyday life. Airship crews were busy, but they were busy *doing* something. City-dwellers, alternatively, seemed to be in a hurry to get somewhere, but little else. Watching them, Zoya felt a pang of longing for her crew-mates. Her friends. She couldn't wait to introduce them to Eva, and show them that Dodsley wasn't all bad, and tell them everything that had happened. She tried to block from her mind thoughts of Cid and his gunshot wound. And Kane, and his penchant for murder. She had to believe her friends were alive, or else what were they trying to save?

Bucker was starting to get restless and making comments about going to look for Dodsley when the thief eventually returned. Draped over his forearm were four sheets of burgundy cloth, which he displayed with a smile. 'You like?'

Eva frowned. 'What are they?'

'Aviation Army uniforms.'

Eva regarded the clothes again, this time a little more

closely. She lifted a flap and spotted the eagle emblem. 'Yes,' she said, smiling. 'Yes!'

'What?' asked Zoya.

'If he's thinking what I'm thinking, the Aviation Army does unannounced searches on moored airships once a day.'

'And?' said Bucker.

'So,' said Dodsley, dropping the uniforms on the lion statue's outstretched paw. 'We dress up as soldiers and tell them it's a search.'

'But we can't fly with Knottingham's men on board!' said Zoya.

Eva chuckled. 'That's why it's such a good idea. When the army performs the searches, the ships' crews have to line up on the platform.'

Zoya nodded. 'Then we fly off.' She laughed. 'Yes.'

'It'll do until a better idea comes along,' said Eva.

Eva led them off—first down one street, then turning at a crossroads and slipping down another. Zoya realized after a while that Eva was leading them towards the towering Constaff building at the centre of the city. From near its base, the building looked like a mountain, solid and massive, daring people to climb. Zoya wasn't surprised Eva had tried to rob it. She'd have done the same, had she been a city thief. As they reached the structure's base, Zoya asked Eva to point out where she'd been caught.

'You can't see it from here. It's round the other side.'

Eva led on, as Zoya jogged to catch up. 'Where are we going, anyway?'

'You saw the air-docks when we came in?'

Zoya thought back to her flight to the aviation museum, and the huge, circular air-docks carved into the city walls. She nodded.

'The docks have to be high in the air so there isn't too much traffic inside the city. But it means every time you want to take an airship ride,' she stopped and gestured at the large crowd that had formed ahead, 'you have to take the elevator.'

The elevator was a huge, brown, metallic disc as big as a building, which rested on four squat pillars in the ground. Nestled beneath the front two pillars was a busy ticket booth. Beyond, a gently sloping staircase led up to the platform. The elevator floor had to be a yard thick, if not more, and skirting its edge was a metal safety railing. Emerging from the centre of the disc was the elevator's cable, a chunky line of intertwined metal filaments that soared into the sky. At its zenith, suspended above the city like pearls on a string, were a dozen air-docks.

'How?' asked Zoya, awestruck.

'Don't ask,' said Dodsley.

'No, seriously.'

'To be honest, I'm not sure,' said Dodsley. 'The docks were built a hundred years or so ago. There are twelve of them, arranged in a big ring around the city. I think they're embedded in the structure of the wall, but you'd have to read about it to be sure.'

'It's crowded,' said Bucker.

'This is nothing,' said Eva. 'You should see it first thing in the morning. People wait an hour.'

Bucker's eyes grew wide.

'If you've got to get up there, you've got to wait.'

'Isn't there another way?' he asked.

'There are staircases on the wall,' said Eva. 'But it takes as long to climb as it does to wait.'

Half an hour passed before they were able to purchase a ticket and ascend the sloping metal stairs. A smartly-dressed man wearing a peaked cap stood by the entrance to the elevator, checking everyone's ticket and smiling for them to proceed once he was satisfied. When they were on board, Bucker grabbed Zoya's hand. 'C'mon,' he said, 'let's get a spot near the edge.'

He guided her away from Eva and Dodsley, who made their way to a row of fixed seats that circled the central cable. When they reached the edge, Bucker stood on tiptoe so that his head poked over the rail. 'It's like being back on the ship.'

'Yes,' said Zoya. 'I was thinking that.'

Below were the heads of hundreds of people, each waiting for a ticket, and beyond, the pebble-beach of the city, a thousand different buildings all at different heights. 'I can't believe we never came down here,' said Zoya. 'It's such a great place.'

'I was born here,' said Bucker, with a twinkle. 'It's bound to be great! Seriously though, the captain hates it. He says it's a den of thieves.'

'I suppose,' said Zoya. 'But there are lots of other people here too.' She gestured around the elevator. 'Like these.'

Bucker nodded in agreement, then hauled himself up to get a better view. To their left, the ticket inspector admitted the last customer, then slammed shut the door and descended the staircase. There had to be two hundred people on board now. After a short while, the floor beneath Zoya's feet started to rumble, and there came the sound of an engine. Moments later, there was a loud crack to her right, an exhalation of steam, and then slowly the elevator started to rise.

'Do you think we could rob the Constaff building?' asked Zoya.

Bucker glanced across. 'Oh yeah, if we had the whole crew. We could clean them out.'

Silence. Thoughts of the crew passed through their minds.

'We're going to . . .'

'Don't worry . . .'

Their words came out at the same time, causing each to stop and stare at the other. Then they burst out laughing, making everyone nearby look. Once they'd calmed down, Bucker smiled and nodded for Zoya to speak. 'Go on.'

'I was just going to say we'll get them. The crew, I mean.'

'I know,' said Bucker. 'Of course we will.'

Zoya laughed. 'How can you be so sure?'

'Because that's what we do. When one of us is in trouble, we're all in trouble. So we rescue them.'

'Except this time there are only four rescuers,' said Zoya.

'Yeah,' said Bucker, 'but one of them's Zoya DeLarose. The greatest swordfighter in the sky.' Bucker leaned in. 'Don't tell my mum I said that.'

Zoya grinned, thinking of Rosie. But the smile quickly shifted to a frown as she recalled Kane and his prison. 'I should have gone for him back at the crash.'

'You couldn't Zo. You're good, but you can't take on dozens on your own.'

'We're going to have to do it on our own now.'

Bucker shrugged. 'If we have to do it on our own, that's the way it is.'

Zoya glanced at Dodsley and Eva. 'No, we're not on our own.'

Bucker smiled. 'No.'

'Do you really think we can do it?' Zoya asked suddenly.

Bucker nodded. 'We've beaten Kane before, remember. We might have caught him by surprise, but we beat him. We can do it again.'

Listening to Bucker, Zoya felt warm inside. She pulled herself back to the lip of the railing. The elevator had risen quite a distance now, so it was closer to the air-docks than the ground. All around, Zoya could see the city wall, and not far above this a galaxy of airships. Now that their view was unobstructed by buildings and cables, she could also see the sky. It was dark grey, wrapped in thick, black clouds that blocked the sun. Off in the distance, towards the mountains, a fork of lightning split the shadows. Zoya looked at the coming storm and shivered.

34

The elevator came to a halt at the air-dock. Inside, Zoya and the others waited while a team of mechanics bustled around the disc. More experienced travellers pushed towards the elevator doors. Moments later, there was a loud, steamy hiss as the rear door opened. Standing outside was another conductor, who ushered passengers down the steps and away.

The air-dock was a giant, open space about the size of a city-block, edged by multiple platforms, against which rested dozens of airships. Overhead, a sloped roof provided some protection against the weather and driving wind. The dock was level with eleven others that ringed the city, all visible in the distance. Beyond these was the city wall. Zoya was close enough now to see Aviation Army soldiers prowling the structure, and watchtowers poking into the sky. Back in the air-dock, connecting the platforms were thin metal walkways that led passengers away from the elevator and out to their ships.

As she walked, Zoya felt the bite of the wind against her neck. She pulled her jacket out of her knapsack and slipped it over her waistcoat. As the walkway gave way to individual platforms, the crowd started to disperse. Zoya managed to extricate herself from the main flow and waited by the side for the others. 'Where now?' she asked, when they arrived.

Eva looked across the dock. 'Knottingham used to leave his ship over at the far end. Let's try there.'

The others nodded. Eva led them towards the nearest connecting walkway, where she chose the emptiest path and started to walk. Aviation Army soldiers, conspicuous by their pristine uniforms, patrolled nearby platforms. Eva was careful to avoid these too, meaning that a ten-minute walk stretched to twenty.

They had nearly reached the furthest platform just as an airship started to pull away. The ship blew a cloud of dust into their faces and sent a shower of rubbish spiralling towards the street below. Zoya shot up her hand to protect her eyes, then peeked through her fingers to watch the craft float out from the platform and zoom away. Within a minute, the airship—as big as the *Dragonfly*—had shrunk to the size of a pin. Zoya glanced to where it had been and spotted another craft hiding behind. This one was a rackety old ship, about half the size of the first, with an antique engine, rotting hull, chipped paint, and enough cracks to sieve flour. To Zoya's right, Eva stared at the ship with a smile.

'Oh no,' said Zoya.

'What?' asked Bucker, trying to work out what he'd missed.

'That's not it, is it?' Zoya asked Eva.

Eva spread her palms as if presenting a flagship. 'Meet the *Ocean's Doom*.'

The others stared at her with grimacing faces. 'Are you kidding?'

'Nope. That's Knottingham's ship.'

'That's not a ship,' said Bucker, 'it's a bucket.'

'Easy,' said Eva, feigning offence. 'I flew this little lady for two years.'

'I'm surprised you're still alive,' said Dodsley.

'Oi!'

Zoya stared at the splintered planks peeling away from the ship's hull. 'Seriously?'

'Yes!'

'But . . . it's . . .' Zoya groped for the word, '. . . ill.'

Eva threw back her head and laughed. 'Trust me,' she said, 'it looks a lot worse than it is. That ship's come through more adventures than most have in a lifetime.'

The others looked again. The ship leaned against the platform like old man. Bucker shook his head. 'Doesn't look like it.'

'Well,' said Eva, clapping her hands, 'it'll have to do. Unless anyone's got a better airship up their sleeves?' She waited for an answer. When none came, she smiled. 'Thought not. Now, I suggest rather than hanging around here talking about how bad it is, we steal the damn thing and get your friends. Does that sound like a plan?'

Zoya nodded.

'In which case, we need to find somewhere to put on these uniforms.'

They found a little staircase leading to the support structure beneath the air-dock and sneaked down. Dodsley scouted around until he found a shielded spot behind a pillar, then they each took turns getting changed. Bucker went first, followed by Dodsley and Eva. Zoya changed last, accepting the bundle of clothes from Dodsley with a wince. 'I never said you'd look good,' he said.

Zoya had never paid much attention to the Aviation Army uniform. Now that she had to, she was mortified. A burgundy peaked cap with velvet decoration, above a burgundy tunic and trousers. Stitched into both the right sleeve and left breast of the tunic was the Aviation Army insignia—a silver eagle, sandwiched between two gold scrolls. Zoya adjusted the clothes as best she could—turning up the hems of her trousers and tunic—then stepped out from behind the pillar.

No sooner had she emerged than Bucker burst out laughing. Zoya frowned. 'You can talk. You look like a choirboy.'

Dodsley spent a few minutes demonstrating an Aviation

Army officer's walk and the way they should stand and talk. Zoya and Bucker had a go, but they struggled to catch the tone. 'They're not going to believe we're Aviation Army anyway,' said Zoya, 'we're too small.'

'Yes,' said Dodsley, 'that was my worry. But we're going to tell them you're recruits in the new academy. They'll believe it or they won't. Either way, we're taking the ship.' He paused to straighten Bucker's posture, pushing a hand into his lower back. 'Leave the talking to me,' he continued. 'I'll keep them occupied. You three need to board the ship. Pretend you're checking it for stolen cargo or something. Really, you need to be looking for the engine. This is an old oil ship, so we need to feed it with oil. When you find it, say the words, "Sir, I think we've found something. You'd better come and have a look." Repeat that so I know you've got it.'

The others repeated the words.

'Good. When you say that, I'm going to board the ship and we're going to get out of there. Then it's up to you, Eva.'

Eva winked. 'Nothing to worry about.'

'Does anyone have any questions?' asked Dodsley.

Bucker and Zoya looked at each other silently.

'We'll be fine,' said Dodsley, waving away their fears. 'You forget, this is what I used to do for a living! Just remember, you're Aviation Army soldiers. You don't take backchat from anyone.' He peered through the grating above his head at the platform, where a few of Knottingham's men were loading the ship. He watched them, then looked down at the others. 'C'mon,' he said, clapping his hands, 'let's go steal an airship.

35

The men on board the *Ocean's Doom* jumped down off the airship and onto the platform as soon as they saw Dodsley marching towards them. All rough and weathered from years in the sky, they stood together as they waited for him to cross the walkway with the others. Eventually, one of the men—a black-haired, muscular man with a gold earring and tanned, stubbly face—stepped away from the others. He folded his arms across his chest. 'What can we do for you officers?'

'Is this the *Ocean's Doom?*' Dodsley asked.

'It might be,' said the man with the earring.

'It either is or it isn't,' said Dodsley. 'Answer the question.'

The man looked at his shipmates, then back at Dodsley. 'Yes.'

'We've come to look at your airship, Mr . . . ?'

'Ronson,' said the man.

'Mr Ronson, my associates are going to board your vessel and make sure you're not harbouring any contraband. That's not likely to be a problem, is it?'

Ronson sighed and shook his head. 'You can't do this. My boss has a deal with the . . .'

Dodsley stopped pacing and walked up so that his face was just a few inches from Ronson's. 'I don't care,' he snapped, 'whether your boss has a deal with the man in the moon. My men are going to look around this ship. Is that clear?'

Ronson frowned.

'Is that clear?'

'Yes.'

'Good,' said Dodsley. He pivoted away from Ronson to face Zoya, Bucker, and Eva. 'Quick as you can then, recruits. Call me at the first sight of something suspicious.'

'Yes sir!' said the others. They walked purposefully up the gangplank, onto the ship, dumped their backpacks and began to root around amongst the cargo. As they worked, Dodsley stood by the men, his back straight and eyes fixed ahead.

'The Aviation Army's sending kids now, are they?' said one of the crew.

'Those are not children,' said Dodsley, eyes remaining forward. 'They are new recruits from the Dalmacian Academy. And that's the last time you insult them.'

'They look like kids,' muttered the man, but he was silenced by a glare from Ronson. On board, Zoya tried to give the impression that she was searching hard amongst the barrels, but in reality her entire focus was on finding the engine.

'They've moved it,' whispered Eva. 'It used to be at the back of the ship. Keep looking.'

Oil engines were about the size of a wardrobe, with metal casing. Zoya looked about the deck, trying to find a corner big enough. Nothing stood out. On the platform, Dodsley showed signs of nerves, tapping his toes on the metal. Behind him, Knottingham's men were discussing something, bunched with their heads together. Zoya watched them briefly, then returned her attention to the deck. She was beneath the mainmast, with Bucker behind and Eva to her left. It was while glancing at Eva that Zoya spotted a structure she'd failed to notice before, just over the older girl's shoulder. It was different to any oil engine she'd seen before, but it was the right size.

Eva spotted the spark in Zoya's eyes, and glanced behind her. 'Interesting,' she whispered. 'Time to fetch Dodsley.'

Zoya ran to the gunwale. 'Sir, I think we've found something. You'd better come and have a look.'

When Dodsley heard the words he stopped tapping his foot, aimed a sharp glare at Ronson, then started to make his way up the gangplank. As he moved, Ronson stepped out from amongst the crew. 'The Dalmacia Academy only opened two months ago.'

Dodsley kept walking. His eyes met Eva's. 'So?'

'So,' said Ronson, 'there couldn't have been any graduates yet.'

On the ship, Zoya froze.

'They're getting experience,' said Eva.

'I don't think so,' said Ronson, looking up. 'I don't think the Aviation Army would send two kids to shake down Severn Knottingham's airship. They're stupid, but they're not that stupid.'

Eva looked down at Dodsley, whose eyes registered panic.

'And if they ain't real Aviation Army, you two aren't either. Which means I don't have to listen to a word you say.'

'Eva,' said Dodsley, 'did you find the engine?'

'Yes.'

'Then I suggest we get out of here,' Dodsley continued, 'because I *think* they're onto us.' With that, he leapt into the ship, before kicking out the wooden gangplank and sending it spinning to the city below.

Back on the platform, Severn's men leapt forward, pulling out knives. One or two backed up, ready to cross the gap that now separated the ship from the platform. Before they could jump, Ronson held out an arm. 'Stay there,' he said. 'Go fetch a new plank. Now!'

On board, Dodsley rose from the deck. 'Time to go, Eva!' he said, passing the pilot. 'Zoya, follow me.'

'I'm trying,' called Eva.

Dodsley led Zoya to the bow, where he reached his hand into a box of apples and handed her one. 'Listen, we've got about two minutes before those men get on board. If they do, we're dead. So they're not going to get on board. Grab anything you can and throw it. Do it as if your life depends on it. Which it does!'

Zoya nodded, tossed the apple, and then started to grab whatever she could from the deck to throw down. She found a few bottles of ale spilling out of a lidless barrel and tossed these down, one-by-one. Few hit their targets. Most whistled past the crew's heads or smashed into the walkway. But the missiles were enough to slow the men down, so Zoya threw as many as she could as fast as she could and prayed for Eva to hurry. Bucker joined her, dragging behind him a sack of carrots. He started to throw them as Zoya felt the rumble of the engine and the ship jerk beneath her feet, lurching her to the left. From somewhere over their shoulders, Dodsley exclaimed. 'Thank god! Let's get out of here!'

Zoya and Bucker dropped their final missiles, then raced to the centre of the deck, where Dodsley was kicking away the planks Knottingham's men were trying to land. Zoya passed him on her way to the bridge, where Eva was standing at the wheel. 'Are you sure you can fly this?' she asked.

'Zoya,' said Eva, offended, 'I can make this little bird dance!'

She gunned the engine and spun the wheel to starboard, causing the ship to shunt upwards and right. The planks set up by Knottingham's men plummeted to the city, and Zoya watched the men grow smaller from up on the bridge, the snarls on their faces sharper and angrier with every yard. She smiled at the sight, a big smile, one so broad it lit up the airship. Pretty soon, the smile became a laugh. She didn't stop as the airship picked up speed, driving through the airdock and into the open sky.

36

A few more minutes passed before Eva and Dodsley started to calm. Dodsley ran across the ship, from starboard to port, bow to stern, springing onto the gunwale and surveying the sky for black smudges, puffs of steam, smoke, anything that might give away an Aviation Army airship, or Knottingham's men. But he saw nothing.

Eventually, he returned to centre-deck, where Zoya and Bucker were sitting cross-legged watching Eva fly. 'I think we're clear.' He ran a hand through his hair. 'How's it going, Eva?'

Eva grimaced. 'She's older than I remember. It's taking me a while to get used to her again.'

'You're doing great,' said Dodsley.

Zoya jumped to her feet. 'I'm going to take a look around. Do you want to come, Buck?'

'I'm OK,' said Bucker. 'I'm going to stay here. There's a storm over there. I want to watch the lightning.'

'Suit yourself,' said Zoya. She made her way to the bow

of the ship, towards the largest cabin on deck. The door was swinging on its hinges, and she slipped inside feeling like she was trespassing. She found herself in the ship's dining hall, and saw a service counter, pots, pans, plates, cutlery, and half a dozen oblong tables. The room was smaller than the *Dragonfly*'s, although only by a little. She weaved past the tables to the back of the hall, through a pair of wooden saloon doors and into a pantry. She breathed a sigh of relief when she realized it was stocked, and started to root through the boxes to see what they had. There was bread, potatoes, rice, onions, garlic, butter, beans, cheese, eggs, some cured meat, tomatoes, green vegetables, spices, fruits. The men of the *Ocean's Doom* could certainly eat.

Zoya picked an apple out of a basket on the shelf, and noticed a hatch to her left in the hall. She gripped the iron handle and hauled it open. In the gap was a wooden ladder that led down to the underbelly of the ship. Zoya snatched an oil lantern from the wall and clambered down. An overwhelming, rotten smell hit her as soon as she placed her feet on the lower deck. Zoya had to pinch her nose to stop from retching. She had always despised the amount of cleaning Vaspine made them do on the *Dragonfly*, but she preferred it to the smell of the *Ocean's Doom* a hundred times over.

Keeping her fingers clamped on her nostrils, Zoya used the lantern to guide her around. She poked her head into grubby sleeping cabins and filthy washrooms. She struggled to find a single bunkroom with a made bed, or one without empty beer bottles and mugs crowding the floor. Nor could she find a single washroom free of dirty underwear and mould. Storm or no storm, Zoya promised herself she'd spend the night up on deck.

There was also an intriguing room at the ship's bow. Zoya almost missed it in the darkness, behind its wall of hanging leather armour. But as she wandered past the armour she spotted something glinting in the lamplight. She pushed aside a few of the tunics and slipped through the gap to a room full of weapons—swords, daggers, crossbows, axes, maces, and spears. Unlike the ship that surrounded them, these weapons were superbly well maintained—sharpened, polished, and each displayed on its own hook.

Zoya picked up and swung some of the swords in an attempt to find a blade with the right balance to replace Storm. The room housed one or two decent weapons, but nothing to match Rosie's gift. Hanging each one back on the wall, she made a note of the armoury's location, then worked her way back up to the deck. 'Find anything?' asked Dodsley, when he saw her.

'Not much,' said Zoya. 'It's pretty grim. But they've got plenty of food. And I found an armoury.'

'An armoury?' Dodsley raised his eyebrows.

Zoya nodded.

'That'll make the raid on Kane easier.' He glanced at Eva, who nodded.

'What do you want me to do now?' asked Zoya.

Dodsley pursed his lips. 'I don't know about you guys, but I'm starving. You could make us some food.'

'Hey,' said Eva, calling down from the bridge. 'What about me?'

'What about you?'

'I'm stuck here.'

Dodsley smiled. 'Don't worry, we'll eat up there with you.' He glanced at the rainclouds then pulled a face.

Zoya started to make her way to the mess hall. She wasn't much of a cook, but she'd picked up a few things from Charlie on the *Dragonfly*. The dish of hers that always garnered praise was a fried-meat and cheese sandwich. Even Zoya had to admit it was something special. She grabbed a loaf of bread, a knob of butter, an onion, and some of the cured meat from the pantry, then found the stove and set to work putting it all together. After a couple of false starts (during which she cremated a pan of onions), she managed to brown the meat, toast the bread, melt the cheese and pile it so high that—even if the sandwich didn't look appetizing—there was at least enough to go around.

Zoya loaded her creation onto a wooden trolley, along with four plates, four mugs, and a jar of water from the barrel at the back of the hall. This, she wheeled out onto the deck.

'Mmm,' said Bucker, smelling the meat. He put down his sweeping brush and followed his nose to the food. 'I think it's time to eat.'

Zoya patted Bucker's hand away as he tried to snatch a slice, before wheeling the trolley all the way to the ship's stern. Eva was still there, locked to the wheel. 'Dinner is served,' said Zoya.

Bucker and Dodsley helped her to carry the food up the steps onto the bridge, then they arranged themselves comfortably on the floor. It had started to rain a few minutes before—big, glistening drops that thudded into the deck and sploshed up around them. None of them minded—least of all Zoya, who wouldn't have relinquished her sandwich in an earthquake. If anything, the lightning provided a form of dinner-time entertainment, and they each found themselves staring at the sky, munching on their food.

Once they'd cleared their plates and drained their mugs, Dodsley carried the pots back to the trolley and deposited them ready for washing. As he returned, he leaned against the wooden rail that surrounded the bridge and fixed his eyes on the others. 'I never thought I'd be here,' he said, after a moment, 'when you set me free of that cage.' He glanced at Zoya. 'If I'm honest, I planned to get rid of you as soon as I found those damned goggles.'

Zoya arched her eyebrows.

'I'm not much of a hero,' continued Dodsley. 'In fact, I

don't think, until these last few days, I'd done a single good deed in my life. But you two do things differently.'

'That's the *Dragonfly* way,' said Zoya.

'I like it,' said Dodsley. 'It feels good to help people, instead of robbing them.'

'Or leaving them hanging from a wire,' chimed in Eva.

Dodsley smiled. 'Or leaving them hanging from a wire.'

'You've really helped us,' said Zoya. 'Thanks.'

'No, I got you into this in the first place,' said Dodsley, waving away her words. 'There's not much honour amongst thieves at the best of times, but you got those goggles fair and square. I should have let you take them. And I knew Kane would have his spies out for your ship as soon as you took me on board. I could have said something.' Dodsley shook his head.

'We all do stupid things,' said Bucker.

'Yeah? Not any more,' said Dodsley.

Zoya glanced up to see Eva smiling. There was a glint in her eye as she regarded Dodsley. 'So what do we do now?'

'I'm going to undo my mistake,' said Dodsley. 'I'm going to rescue Zoya's friends.'

Zoya pushed herself up off the deck and laid a hand on the thief's shoulder. 'I never told you why I stole the goggles, did I?'

'It doesn't matter,' said Dodsley.

'It does. The reason I wanted the goggles so badly was because I'd forgotten to get a present for my friend's birthday.

221

I was scared to own up, so I went to steal something I had no right stealing and ended up putting everybody in danger. If you're to blame, so am I. I've got a mistake to fix. And I tell you what, this time I'm going to put an end to Kane once and for all.'

Dodsley smiled, pulled Zoya towards him, and rubbed her hair. 'And you two?' he looked at Bucker and Eva.

Bucker leapt to his feet. 'Of course I'm in. Kane's got my mum. Nobody takes my mum.'

Zoya detached herself from Dodsley and put up a hand for Bucker to high-five. Now, all eyes were on Eva, who'd remained quiet at the wheel. When she realized they were all looking at her, she turned her head slowly and stared at Dodsley. 'Are you sure we can do this? Are you sure we're not leading these children to their deaths?'

Dodsley approached her. 'I've never been more sure of anything.'

Eva inhaled once, pursed her lips, and shook her head. 'Damn, Dodsley Brown. You'd better be right.' And she returned to the wheel and set a course for the Island in the Sky.

37

'Let me have a look,' said Bucker.

'Wait,' said Zoya, adjusting her binoculars.

Bucker sighed. 'OK, tell me what you see . . .'

Zoya and Bucker were lying on their bellies at the edge of a grassy promontory, sandwiched between Dodsley and Eva, also on their fronts. Surrounding the four was a web of bushes and trees that Zoya hoped concealed them from anyone watching. The promontory formed part of a ridge to the south of the Island in the Sky that stretched for a mile behind them, gradually giving way to the island's only town, Moonfall. Ahead, the ridge dropped into a dense forest, beyond which lay a shallow lake and a huge, stone fortress.

'It's . . . big,' said Zoya. 'There are . . .' she counted in her head, 'twelve cannons on the wall nearest us and . . .' she counted again, 'nine guard towers.'

'Nine?' Bucker repeated the word. 'Nine?'

'Ahuh.'

'What else?'

Zoya drew breath. 'There are . . . men everywhere. And transporters. Patrolling the sky.'

'How big is it?' asked Bucker.

'I don't know. There's a massive moat around the outside, then a wall, then a bunch of buildings.'

'Any more weapons?'

Eva shot Bucker a look. 'What, more than men and cannons and guard towers?'

'There's a tall structure in the middle,' said Zoya, fiddling with the binoculars to improve their focus. 'It's higher than everything else.'

'Describe it,' said Eva.

'It's the prison,' said Dodsley.

The others looked at him as he lowered his binoculars. 'When you have prisoners that important, you'd set most of your men to guard them, yes?'

Eva shrugged. 'I guess.'

'Zoya, how many men are there around that central block?'

Zoya shifted the binoculars so she was staring at the block. It was a square building in the centre of the fortress, slightly taller than the wall surrounding it. Ringing the block— halfway up its walls—was a metal walkway crowded with guards. 'Loads,' she said. 'Just, loads!'

'See,' said Dodsley. 'I can't think of anything else they'd be hiding in there.'

'Let's go then,' said Bucker, jumping to his feet. 'What are we waiting for?'

'It's not that easy,' said Dodsley.

Eva pulled the binoculars gently from Zoya's face and laid them in her lap. She swung herself upright so she was sitting cross-legged. 'Why?'

Dodsley rubbed his eyes. 'This is the reason I didn't want to come here. You see, I know about this place. I've heard guys in Mika's talking about pirates who've tried to raid it. There's a lot of money in there.' He nodded at the fortress. 'Do you know how many succeeded?'

The others remained quiet.

'Zero. Kane's got that place wrapped up tight. And these guys were good thieves. And there were dozens of them. There are only four of us. We wouldn't stand a chance.'

'What was all that back at the airship then?' asked Bucker. 'Why have we bothered?'

'Hang on,' said Dodsley. 'I'm not saying we can't get your friends. I'm just saying we have to be smart.'

'We are,' said Zoya. 'We're scoping the place out.'

'That's not what I mean,' said Dodsley. He gestured towards the fortress. 'If we fly in, they're going to shoot us out of the sky before we get past the wall. If we try to walk in, they'll cut us down before we get out of the moat. If we try to con our way in, they'll see right through us and kill us on the spot. This isn't Severn Knottingham, it's Kane. You two of all people should know what he's capable of.' He aimed his last words at Zoya and Bucker.

'What about if we walk back to town and hire some men?' said Bucker. 'Lots of them. And we'll get some weapons for the airship.'

'This isn't Dalmacia,' said Dodsley. 'This is the Island in the Sky. The men you're talking about are the worst scumbag sky thieves in the world, probably more loyal to Kane than they ever would be to you. Besides, we don't have any money. What are we going to pay them with?'

'Let's sneak in then,' said Zoya. 'We find a way through the wall, get to Vaspine and the crew, let them out, and fight our way free.'

Dodsley dismissed the idea. 'Too risky. It takes only one of us to get caught and the game's up.'

Zoya slumped.

'We'll head in at night then,' said Eva. 'There's no way they'll see us.'

Dodsley sighed. 'Would you stick lanterns on the fortress wall at night if it was your place?'

Eva pursed her lips. 'Yes.'

'Then so would Kane.'

'What can we do then?' asked Zoya. She moved away and leaned against a nearby tree trunk, racking her brain. She longed to speak to the captain, to know he was OK, to know they were all OK, that Rosie was keeping her spirits up, that

226

Cid was still smoking his pipe. An image of the last time she'd seen Cid flashed into her mind, face-down on the deck of the *Dragonfly*, a deep, red patch growing on his back. The way he'd stepped forward made her want to cry. But it also made her angry—angry with Kane, and anyone who'd ever joined him in terrorizing the sky.

She turned back to the others, who hadn't moved. Eva spread her palms to indicate she had nothing. Dodsley, too, was deep in thought, his thumb and forefinger on the bridge of his nose. Only Bucker seemed close to something. He jumped to his feet. 'Eva,' he said, 'how high can the *Ocean's Doom* go?'

'What do you mean?'

'Vaspine never let us fly very high in the *Dragonfly*, but I know it could go a lot higher than we ever did. How high can the *Ocean's Doom* go?'

Eva inhaled. 'I don't know. I never took it that high.'

'Could it get above the clouds?' asked Bucker.

Eva laughed. 'Oh yes. All airships can.'

'What's your idea, Buck?' asked Dodsley, sitting up.

'We need to get to that block, that's what everyone's saying, yes? That's where the prison is?'

Dodsley nodded.

'But we can't fly in from here and we can't sneak in and we can't hire anyone?'

'Go on,' said Dodsley.

'So where's the one place they wouldn't expect us to come from?'

Zoya narrowed her eyebrows. 'Underground?'

'No.'

Silence. Each thought for a while. Then Eva jumped to her feet. 'From above!'

'Yes!' Bucker grinned. 'They won't expect us from above. And they won't see us coming either. Why don't we fly really high and drop straight down like a stone, enter through the roof?'

Catching the flow of Bucker's thoughts, Dodsley, too, jumped to his feet. He wagged a finger in excitement. 'I get it, little man. I get it. But why not take it further? We don't need that rackety old airship once we're in, do we?'

Bucker shrugged. 'As long as they've got something to get us home.'

'They must have,' said Zoya.

'I agree,' said Dodsley. 'And if that's true, I say we use Knottingham's ship as a weapon, hit them hard. Instead of just entering from above and waiting for them to shoot us, we'll crash straight into the heart of the lair and they won't even see us coming. Imagine the confusion. We'd be able to slip by and rescue everyone while they're still trying to work out what's going on.'

Zoya looked at Dodsley. 'Are you mad? The *Dragonfly*'s crew's in there.'

'We don't have to hit anything,' protested Dodsley, 'just bring it down in the courtyard. We bail before it crashes, land safely in parachutes and we're inside. Then we go and get your friends.'

'It's got an oil engine,' said Zoya. 'It'll explode.'

'Yes!' said Dodsley. 'That's what we want. Flaming wood everywhere. The more chaos the better. The reason no-one ever gets into this place is because they walk right up to the front door and knock. We're going to smash it to pieces. It'll work, I'm sure of it.' Dodsley glanced at the others. 'Well?'

Bucker laughed. 'Sounds like something the captain would do. I'm in!'

Zoya rubbed her face with her hands. 'Wow, I don't know. Can we do it, even?'

Dodsley deflected the question to Eva. She considered it, then spoke. 'No. Oh maybe, I don't know.' She clapped her hands in frustration. 'We'd have to get very high to stop them seeing us coming. And even if we can, there'll still be a hundred men inside. We need something better . . .'

'Can we get the ship in place?' said Dodsley. 'Can you *do* it?'

Eva gritted her teeth, then shook her head in defeat. 'Yes!' she said. 'Yes! Of course I can. I'll crash us into anything you want. It's the stupidest thing anyone's ever asked me to do, but I'll do it!'

'That's more like it. And don't worry about what we're going to do when we're inside. Leave that to me.'

'I was planning to,' said Eva.

Dodsley gestured for the others to come together. They stood close, each holding the arm of the person next to them. 'Is everyone sure,' he asked, 'because once we do this there's no turning back?'

Zoya bared her teeth. 'He's got my family. And Bucker's. I'm going to end this today.'

Bucker and Eva nodded too. Dodsley shook their arms. 'Good,' he said. 'Then let's go crash an airship.'

38

Dodsley led the way back to the airship, which they'd concealed behind a rocky outcrop a mile or so from the ridge. When they arrived, they headed off in separate directions to prepare—Bucker to check the weather, Dodsley to check their armour, and Eva to prepare the ship for its last journey. Zoya had something to do, too, and she made her way to the makeshift quarters she'd arranged near the stern.

It was hot in the cabin. Zoya collapsed on her bed and lay there, breathing in the hot air, before pushing herself upright and unclipping her father's locket, watching it dangle from her fingers.

'You've done a lot for me over the years,' she whispered, taking the locket in her hand. 'You've got me out of some scrapes. I've not had to ask a lot recently, but I'm going to ask for something today. See, some of my friends are in trouble. In fact, apart from the people on this ship, I'd say about all of my friends are in trouble. And us four are the only ones who can get them out.' She paused. 'But it's not going to be easy. We've got a lot to do, and Kane's mad, and his men are going to try to stop us.' She paused again, breathed deeply. 'I know the captain says we shouldn't rely on luck, but I think we're going to need some today. So I'm asking you for a bit of help.' She opened her eyes and looked down at the locket. 'Please.'

Zoya kissed the pendant and hooked it around her neck. Then she swung herself off the bed, ready to go. She returned to the deck sporting a broad smile, and saw Dodsley first, returning from the armoury, kitted out in leather mail with two daggers swinging at his side. 'You look like a Titan,' she said. Zoya made her way to the armoury, where she found Bucker. As soon as he saw her, he grabbed her arm and led her to the wall of swords. 'You've got to see this. I found one that's perfect for you,' he said. 'Just like Storm.' He lifted a weapon from the top row. It was one Zoya hadn't spotted, its blade dull and plain.

'It definitely looks like Storm,' said Zoya, taking a couple of swipes. 'Feels like it too.'

'Told you.'

'What are you taking?'

'I found these,' said Bucker. He pulled out a pair of daggers similar to the ones Zoya had seen Dodsley with.

'Oh, I see the boys are sticking together.'

'We've all got to stick together,' said Bucker.

232

Zoya scanned the armoury to see if Bucker had missed anything useful, but he hadn't. Plucking a scabbard from the wall, she swung it around her waist and strapped her new sword in. It felt strange to have a weapon by her side again.

The weapon room was a mess now, covered with the armour Dodsley had tossed down as he sifted through it. Almost everything was too big for Zoya and Bucker, but by going through every last piece they were able to find a few that fitted. They spent the next five minutes slipping into these, making sure they were secure. When Zoya had finished strapping on Bucker's last chest plate, she couldn't help but laugh. 'You look like an elf.'

'You look like a beer barrel,' said Bucker.

Zoya glanced down at the leather plate encircling her chest and agreed. A moment's silence passed as they stared at each other in the dim light, then Bucker frowned. 'Zoya, is this a good idea?'

'The armour?'

'No. The rescue.'

'What do you mean?'

'I mean, are we going to be able to do this? What happens if something goes wrong and we can't jump to safety? Or if Kane sees us and shoots us down? What happens if he catches us when we're on the ground? Then we're all trapped. Or dead.'

This final word caught in Bucker's throat, and he dropped his gaze. Zoya knew how he was feeling. 'I'm scared too, you know? I feel like we did before we sneaked onto the *Shadow*.'

'That was scary,' said Bucker.

'And I don't know about any of the things you said. All of them might happen, maybe worse. But I do know this: we've got to go. You can't ever let fear stop you from doing anything, because it's like a disease. You let it stop you once, and it'll stop you next time. And the next time. Eventually you'll be too afraid to move! Besides,' continued Zoya, punching him playfully in the shoulder, 'what would the captain do?'

'Come and get us,' said Bucker.

'And Cid?'

'He'd come and get us too.'

'And your mum?'

Bucker laughed. 'She'd tell us off. But before that she'd come and get us.'

'Exactly,' said Zoya. 'So the way I see it, we don't have a choice.'

Bucker thought, then nodded in agreement. 'C'mon then,' he said, heading back towards the deck. 'If we're going to do it, let's get it over with.'

'Yes captain!' said Zoya, and she followed him out the door.

39

Eva was already out on deck when the kids arrived, putting the finishing touches to her own armour. Zoya jogged over to help her tighten the straps. When they were finished, Eva jumped into a fighting stance. 'How do I look?'

'You look ace,' said Zoya.

'Are you two ready?'

Zoya glanced at Bucker, who nodded. 'We're ready.'

'Me too,' said Dodsley, approaching from behind. 'Let's get it over with.' In his hands, he carried three canvas backpacks. Out of each swung a cord, like the parachutes back on the *Dragonfly*. 'I found these,' he said. 'Should allow us to get to the ground safely.'

'Erm,' said Eva. 'There are only three.'

'I know,' said Dodsley. 'It's all I can find. Looks like you two are going to have to drop in together. You OK with that?' He glanced at Zoya and Bucker.

'I guess.'

'Good. In which case, I think we're ready.'

Eva flicked a switch on the bridge, sending a rumble through the belly of the ship. She waited until the engine had caught, then revved to give it some power. 'It's going to take a lot of oil to get us as high as we need to go. Zoya, you can look after that.' Eva pointed to a transparent tube built into the engine, half-filled with black gunk. 'When it falls below this mark,' she pointed to a line an inch below the gauge's current level, 'empty an entire canister from that pile into the funnel. Make sense?'

Zoya looked at the pile of rusty canisters next to the gunwale and nodded.

'You can't take your eyes off it for a second,' said Eva, 'or we'll start to lose altitude and there'll be nothing I can do to stop us.'

Zoya nodded again.

'Dodsley, Bucker,' she turned to the boys, 'you'll be my eyes. I'm not going to be able to see below us up on the bridge, so I need you to look out from the gunwale and tell me when we're directly above the fortress. Yes?'

'Yes,' they said, then they bounded off to keep watch. Eva leapt into position behind the wheel, then reached down to the throttle. The ship lurched forwards and started to rise into the sky. Soon, they'd reached normal cruising height, at which point Eva nudged the airship forwards and started a gentler, angled climb. From her spot next to the gunwale, Zoya spied the ridge from which they'd scoped out the fortress, then the forest, the lake beyond that and Kane's lair. She peeked at the oil gauge, but it had barely moved. So far, so good.

'OK, Kane's place is directly ahead,' said Dodsley.

'Got it,' said Eva. She was shouting to be heard above the wind, leaning into the wheel. 'I'm going to have to put some power into it, so things might get a bit bumpy. Hold onto something.'

Zoya gripped a handrail on the engine as the airship thrust forward. She was higher than she'd ever been—the ground below blurred into a tapestry of greens and browns. The ship continued to ascend for another minute, Dodsley and Bucker calling out course corrections, until Zoya glanced down at the oil gauge and realized it was low. She took a deep breath, let go of the engine and staggered to the canisters. She made it without tripping, gripped the gunwale with one hand and bent over to gather up the nearest can. As she made her way back, the ship started to splutter and judder.

'Zoya,' shouted Eva, 'get some oil in there now!'

Zoya tugged hard at the canister's cap. It didn't move. She glanced at the oil gauge and groaned. 'C'mon.' Sliding her fingers beneath the cap, she pulled once more, wrenching the skin. This time, the lid came away. Zoya ignored the pain and positioned the canister above the funnel, emptying its contents inside. An agonizing moment followed in which the oil appeared to do nothing, then the engine stopped spluttering and started to rumble once more.

Zoya breathed properly for the first time in a minute. She collapsed into the gunwale and looked over the top. They were above the clouds now, and the birds too. A flock soared and dipped beneath them. Zoya spied the lake she and the others had seen from the ridge, and ahead of that Kane's fortress—a solid, grey square. 'How much higher?' she yelled.

'Not far,' said Eva.

The airship lurched again, tossing Zoya into the gunwale. To her right, she heard a scream and looked across just in time to see Bucker crash to the ground, his head bouncing off the deck. Zoya shrieked. Dodsley had also spotted Bucker's fall, and he dropped to the deck to make his way over. 'Leave it!' yelled Zoya. 'I'll go.' Dodsley rose reluctantly as Zoya released her grip on the gunwale and started to make her way across. She reached Bucker and rolled him over. For a moment, he lay motionless. Then Zoya cried in relief as he shook his head and lifted a hand to the bump that was already forming on his temple.

'Ouch.'

'Hang on, you two,' said Eva, ducking to avoid a flying canister. 'It'll ease in a second.'

The roar of the wind was deafening, and the airship creaked like it could tear apart at any moment. Somewhere amongst the noise, Zoya heard a crack that was too loud for comfort, and instinctively opened her eyes. Above, the mainmast had snapped in half, prevented from falling only by the netting that surrounded it. Zoya watched the beam stretch the ropes, snapping them like threads, before it sliced through the last one and plummeted to the deck. Before she could think, she grabbed Bucker and rolled them both away as the beam crashed into the deck. 'Evaaaaaaaa!' yelled Zoya.

'We're nearly there!' shouted Eva.

The airship continued to judder for another few seconds, then, as if they'd emerged onto a tranquil ocean, the shaking stopped, the wind ceased, and the four of them were left on deck in silence. Zoya felt her heartbeat in her ears. 'Is that it?'

'That's it,' said Eva.

Zoya helped Bucker to his feet, then pushed herself up and sucked in a few lungfuls of air. She stumbled to the gunwale and peered over the edge. They were so high now Zoya could see the entire shape of the Island in the Sky below—a truncated oval, with her father's mountain at one end and green meadows at the other. The large lake in the centre was a blue-black smudge, while the buildings of Moonfall were mere dots. Despite its reputation as a den of sky thieves, the island looked beautiful from above.

Returning to centre-deck, Zoya breathed in deep one more time. The air felt light at that height, and she fought hard to fill her lungs. It was eerie too—quiet—like being underwater. Apart from Bucker's breathing to her left and the creaking of the wheel as Eva nudged it left and right, the airship was silent—no wind, no birds, no flapping sails. Somewhere off to her left, Dodsley spoke, but his voice sounded different, muffled. 'Everyone OK?'

'I'm OK,' she said.

'Me too,' said Bucker, rubbing his head.

'Eva?' asked Dodsley.

'I'm OK.'

Dodsley gestured towards the airship. 'She's taken a battering. Can you still steer her into the fortress?'

Zoya looked around. The ship was hurting. The mainmast had collapsed completely, bringing along many of the smaller masts, one or two of which had smashed into the gunwale, leaving gaping holes. Cross-hatched across the deck were dark tracks where the decking had come loose. Scattered over the rest of the deck was every other object not nailed down—barrels, bread, rice, potatoes, ropes, crates, buckets.

'To be honest,' said Eva, patting the wheel, 'I can't believe she made it up here. There's more to her than meets the eye.'

'Will she make it down?' repeated Dodsley.

'Yes,' said Eva. 'We just need to make sure we hold on.'

Dodsley smiled. 'Well then, it's been an honour.' He tossed Eva her parachute, then Zoya and Bucker theirs. Taller than Bucker, Zoya slung the chute over her back, strapped herself in and then opened her arms so Bucker could back into her chest. When he was in position, she fed his arms through the straps and tightened both so they were locked together. She pushed Bucker away to see if the straps would hold. 'Seems secure,' she said.

The four stood, chutes on their backs and strange grins on their faces, each privately wondering how they came to be thousands of yards high, about to purposefully crash an airship into the base of the world's most vicious sky thief. They caught each other's eyes, until eventually, all centred on Eva, still on the bridge.

She smiled broadly, said, 'Good luck,' then snapped the throttle.

The airship hung in the air, then slowly, slowly, started to fall.

40

For a little while, the ship fell straight down, unperturbed by bumpy air, so their view remained much as it had before. Then, suddenly, the airship crashed into a pressure-pocket and lurched sideways, sending it into a spin. From somewhere to her right, Zoya heard Dodsley yell, 'Hold on! Don't let go!' as the ship spun so that its deck was now vertical. Strapped together, Zoya and Bucker clung to what was left of the mainmast, their fingers locked around the pole, their faces pressed up against the deck, bodies dangling below. Every so often, the airship lurched in a new direction, banging them into the deck.

'Are you OK?' called Zoya to Bucker. He groaned.

The airship's spin intensified until it was rotating every ten seconds. Presently, it was upside down, so that Zoya and Bucker had to shift their hands around the mast to maintain their grip. Ahead, Eva was visible through a spider's web of netting, her right arm hooked through the wheel and her left gripping a spoke. When she spotted Zoya, she smiled a half-smile, then quickly returned her attention to staying alive.

To Zoya's right, Dodsley was faring significantly worse, having lost his grip on the metal clamp he'd been using to hold on. He hung by a single rope now, tied loosely to a hook in the ship's side. The rope was long, and it whipped Dodsley wildly, banging him into the gunwale, then the deck, then a mast, then the gunwale again. Each time, he slipped further down the rope. Zoya pointed out what was happening to Bucker, then shouted above the wind. 'We need to get over there!'

Before Bucker could respond, the ship careened into a new pocket of air and jerked violently down. The movement wrenched the rope from Dodsley's hand and sent him tumbling from the ship, over Zoya's shoulder. She screamed as she watched him disappear, straining against Bucker's body, twisting left and right to try to spot Dodsley's parachute. But it was no good. He was gone.

The airship was falling fast now. Zoya made out the fast-approaching grey blocks of Kane's fortress. She steeled herself, ready to let go and pull their parachute cord. Eva spotted this from across the deck. 'Not yet!' she yelled. 'Ten more seconds!'

Zoya shouted the seconds into the wind—her voice a whisper against the torrent—then she and Bucker released

243

their grips and kicked themselves away from the ship into the open air. Above them, Zoya spotted Eva, who'd done the same. Eva's parachute snapped open, then Zoya lost her against the oval of white. Zoya fumbled around her shoulder for their cord, then yanked it hard. For a terrible instant, the cord did nothing. Then, above their heads, came the familiar snap of the fabric and she and Bucker jerked up. 'You OK?' she shouted.

'I think,' said Bucker, his eyes wide.

It was quiet under the canopy, and the image of the airship accelerating to the ground seemed strangely distant. Zoya watched it fall, crashing down inside Kane's fortress close to the prison block. The oil engine exploded on impact, sending an orange-black fireball into the sky, dangerously close to her parachute. Below, the ship disintegrated, sending wooden planks, splinters, metal brackets, and lengths of rope fizzing off in every direction. Some of this climbed as high as Zoya and Bucker, so they had to shield themselves with their arms. After a few seconds, the fireball began to recede and Zoya was able to see what remained of their airship—a crumpled heap of shattered wood and metal. Chunks of the vessel had landed hundreds of yards from the main body, so that small fires burned as far as Zoya could see.

They were close to the ground now and Zoya shifted her attention to landing. She spied a good spot off to their left—a small patch of grass around the back of a dividing wall. Zoya communicated this plan to Bucker, then together they used their weight to steer the parachute in the right direction. They landed safely. However, no sooner had Zoya managed to unhook herself than Eva came streaming in. She crashed into them feet-first, sending all three sprawling. They tumbled together for a few yards, trying to escape, before eventually Zoya managed to tear herself free. She waited for the others to stop rolling, then helped Eva out from under her canopy and pulled Bucker upright.

'Where's Dodsley?' asked Eva.

'He got thrown off when we were still quite high,' said Zoya. 'He had his chute, though.'

All three looked up. Sure enough, drifting in above the central block was a black dot. Above that, hung a white parachute. Zoya smiled to see him safe, but her smile melted quickly when she realized Dodsley's parachute was tangled. He was approaching the ground at an awkward angle, moving fast. 'He's not going to be able to control that,' said Eva. 'We need to get over there.'

Keeping their eyes on Dodsley, they checked their weapons, then ran out from their hiding place behind the wall. A wide courtyard stood between them and the crashed airship now, which was itself a hundred yards from the central block. Even at a distance, Zoya could feel the heat of the fire on her skin. She put up a hand to protect her eyes. 'Is he down?'

'Yes,' said Eva. 'The other side of the ship. Let's go.'

Eva led them off, making sure to keep large pieces of debris between them and Kane's men. As they moved, Zoya clamped a hand around the hilt of her sword. 'There don't seem to be many people out here,' she said between breaths.

'No,' said Eva.

They looped around the airship so they approached it from behind. Ahead, lay a wide, clear courtyard. To their left, beside a mound of burning rope, was a dark lump on the floor. The lump was surrounded by a patch of white fabric. 'Dodsley,' said Eva.

Eva sprinted towards Dodsley; Zoya and Bucker followed a few paces behind. They'd made it to within a dozen yards, when two of Kane's men, carrying buckets of water, emerged from a nearby door. The men pulled up as soon as they saw Dodsley's parachute, then froze when they spotted Eva, Zoya, and Bucker. Instantly, the men dropped their buckets and drew their weapons—one a sword and the other a curved dagger. 'I'll deal with these,' said Eva, 'you two check on Dodsley.' Zoya moved to argue, but Eva pushed her away. 'Go!'

Zoya shook her head, then grabbed Bucker's arm and dragged him away. Behind them, they heard a clash of swords as Eva set to work. Zoya resisted the urge to watch, and instead concentrated on removing the canopy from Dodsley. It took them a few moments to find the edges, and more to peel them back. When they finally worked it loose, they found him underneath. He lay unconscious, his face bloodied by a deep cut above his left eye. Another ran from his chin to his collar bone, this too seeping blood. Zoya shared a worried glance with Bucker. Behind her, she heard the patter of Eva's fighting steps, then the sound of a sword as it thrust into human flesh. A moment later, the pilot arrived at her side. 'Nice one!' said Zoya.

'I can eat guys like that for breakfast.' Eva nodded at Zoya's hands. 'How is he?'

Zoya looked down and almost cried out in joy when she realized Dodsley was blinking himself awake. She reached into her back pocket for a handkerchief to wipe away the blood from his face. After a few seconds, Dodsley came around enough to realize where he was, and he pushed Zoya's hands away. 'Are we here?' he asked, sitting bolt upright.

'Yes,' said Eva. 'I'm not sure you are though. How many fingers am I holding up?'

Dodsley rubbed his eyes. 'I'll be fine,' he said. He shook his head. 'I think.' He glanced at the fire. 'What happened?'

'It's the airship,' said Bucker.

Dodsley climbed unsteadily to his feet and brushed down his clothes. He looked at the fire, then around the courtyard to get his bearings. 'Where are Kane's men? This place was jammed yesterday.'

'Getting water to put the fires out?' suggested Eva.

Dodsley shook his head. 'No. That airship signals our presence, and Kane knows why we're here. No, they'll be getting ready to fight. Which means we need to get into the prison now. If we don't free your crew-mates before they get their act together, we don't stand a chance.'

41

'That's not going to be easy,' said Eva. She gestured towards the prison, where a huge chunk of the airship's hull had landed outside the main entrance. 'We'd need a dozen of us to move that.'

Dodsley opened his mouth to speak, but Zoya cut him off. 'Wait. When me and Bucker were chuting in, I spotted a piece of the airship had crashed into the prison wall. We might be able to get in there.'

The others looked amongst each other, then Dodsley shrugged. 'It'll have to do.' He patted himself down to make sure he had everything, then nodded for Zoya to lead on. Zoya took a last glance at the *Ocean's Doom*, then headed in the direction of the central prison block.

They arrived to find more objects from the crash scattered about the building—sections of the gunwale, a length of rope, a wooden spoon, a shattered plate, a couple of mangled oil canisters. Zoya picked her way through the debris to where the hull jutted out from the side of the prison. The wood had crashed through the metal walkway, tearing the rail in half so that a section hung down in an inverted L-shape. Zoya glanced at the rail, then beyond to the hole in the wall. Flames flickered in the gap, sending out thick curls of smoke. Zoya tried to peer into the building, but it was too dark. She turned to the others.

'The crew has to be in there. And I think that rail will get us inside.' She nudged Dodsley. 'Can you reach it?'

Dodsley steadied himself, then leapt up. He missed the rail by a foot.

'Jump on his shoulders,' suggested Eva.

Zoya looked up at the rail, then nodded. 'Yeah. You boost me.' She stepped over to Dodsley. 'I'll grab it.'

Dodsley shrugged, then bent over. As he did, they heard a shout over their shoulders. 'There they are!'

Zoya turned just in time to see three of Kane's men emerge from behind the flaming airship. Immediately, the men started to charge towards them, swords raised above their heads. Eva spotted them a second after Zoya and drew her own weapon. 'Leave them to me and Bucker. You two get that rail down.'

Zoya glanced one last time at Bucker and Eva, then jumped up and edged along Dodsley's back until she was on his shoulders. With a groan, Dodsley straightened himself and sent Zoya high into the air. Reaching up, she gripped the metal rail, then kicked her legs to tell Dodsley to let go. Dodsley unhooked himself, then ran to join Bucker and Eva in the fight. Zoya was left hanging from the rail, her legs dangling five feet above the ground. The metal was hot, and she resisted the urge to let go as she pulled herself up and then drove her weight to the ground. Her momentum caused a stretch of the walkway to slump, dropping to the ground with a clank.

The fall knocked Zoya's breath out of her, and she writhed on the floor for a full minute forcing air into her lungs. When she eventually made it to her feet, ready to join the fight, she realized that Bucker, Dodsley, and Eva had already dispatched Kane's men. 'All right missy,' kidded Dodsley, 'you can put your sword away!'

The hanging rail gave them a direct route up to the second level. Soon, all four were standing on what remained of the walkway. The hull was just a few yards away, flames climbing up its side, black smoke shrouding them. Zoya stepped cautiously through the smoke until she could see the hole that led into the prison. She sidestepped through this, being careful to avoid the flames. The others followed, emerging into a narrow, dark corridor. This, too, was blanketed in smoke, making Zoya cough. She tore a length of fabric from the front of her shirt and used it to cover her mouth. The others found ways to do the same. 'We're not at the top,' she said, voice muffled. 'We need to go up one more level.'

Zoya turned her back and started to cut through the smog. For the first few steps, it was so thick that she had to hold a hand out in front to stop herself from banging into anything. After this, the smoke started to clear and she was able to see where they were going for the first time. They were walking down a long corridor that ran until it hit the end of the building, then turned left. Lining the corridor's inner wall was a series of thin, horizontal windows that looked into the prison.

Inside, it was dark, though a few chunks of flaming airship had crashed through the roof and were providing just enough light to see. The building was a perfect square, with a large atrium in the centre and three levels of corridors around the outside. Each corridor ended in a staircase that led to the next level, and each held rooms that jutted into the central atrium, supported by stone pillars. Zoya glanced down to the floor, then up at the level above. The top floor was different to the others, sporting an open walkway like the one outside. Zoya traced this around the building, searching for some sign of Kane or his men. Instead, she spotted a line of glinting columns in the far corner. There, reflecting in the firelight, were the metal bars of a jail cell.

'I've found them,' called Zoya. 'They're up there!'

Zoya pushed herself away from the window and started to sprint down the corridor towards the stairwell. She bounded up the steps two at a time, then glanced over her shoulder.

She gestured for the others to hurry, then raced along the walkway towards the cells.

As she arrived, she spotted a guard standing between her and the cell. The guard saw Zoya at exactly the same moment, and fumbled in his holster for his gun. Zoya doubled her speed and pulled out the dagger she'd strapped to her leg. She reached the guard and hit him on the temple with the weapon's hilt. He slumped to the floor without a sound, leaving Zoya alone in the centre of the walkway, her pulse thumping.

She waited in silence, not daring to turn around. Then, suddenly, buzzing through the quiet, she heard a voice. It was a deep voice, one Zoya recognized as she recognized her own. 'Zoya DeLarose,' it said. 'Damn good to see you, girl.'

Zoya turned around. Peeking out from behind the metal bars of his jail, was Captain Carlos Vaspine.

42

Zoya had never seen the captain look so tired. Beneath his left eye he had a deep, red bruise that could be seen by the light of the fragments of fire nearby. His clothes were torn and hung loosely from his shoulders. His normally clean-shaven cheeks had a few days' worth of stubble, and his moustache had grown longer than usual, drooping to his chin. Behind him, his crew looked just as broken—exhausted and desolate. Zoya peered into the darkness for Cid and Rosie, but they were nowhere to be seen.

'You sure know how to make an entrance,' said Vaspine.

'I learned from the best,' said Zoya.

Before Vaspine could speak, another face appeared in the light. It was pale, with red eyes from days of tears. Rosie. 'Where is my boy?' she asked. 'Where's Bucker?'

'I'm here, Mum,' said Bucker, stepping forward.

Rosie stared at him without speaking, then burst into tears and thrust her hands through the bars to pull him close.

Vaspine shook his head in admiration. 'How did you survive?' he asked Zoya. 'How did you even get here?'

'I don't know. I really don't. But I'm glad we did.'

'Me too,' said the captain. 'Listen, you need to get us out before more of Kane's men come. Check the guard, he's got a key.'

Zoya hopped over and searched the guard. She found a bunch of keys on a chain around his waist. Unclipping the chain, she took it over to the cell and tried the keys one at a time. As she worked, she glanced over her shoulder to check nobody was coming. Dodsley and Eva, also keeping watch, nodded for her to continue.

'C'mon,' said Vaspine.

Zoya tried a few more keys, the last of which slotted perfectly into the lock and twisted open. Vaspine pushed open the door and gestured for the rest of the crew to get outside. A procession of ragged thieves followed, all cut and bruised, their clothes torn. Hobbling at the back, assisted by the Doc, was the ship's pilot, Cid Lightfoot. As soon as Zoya saw him, she raced over to hug him. However, before she could throw out her arms, Cid shooed her away.

'You're alive!' said Zoya.

'Of course I am,' he said. 'It'd take more than a bullet to get rid of me.' As he said this, Cid pointed down to his chest, where his blood-stained clothes still told the tale of his wound.

'Will he be OK?' Zoya asked the Doc.

'How the hell should I know?'

Cid silenced the Doc with a look. 'I'm fine. I just need to get this goddamned bullet out, that's all.'

Zoya smiled. 'I'm glad you're OK.'

'We're not out of the woods yet,' said Vaspine. 'We're still in the middle of Kane's base. Did you bring a ship?'

Zoya grimaced. 'We did . . .' she paused, thinking of how best to put it, 'but we crashed it.'

Vaspine stared at her, then shook his head.

'It was the only way,' said Dodsley. 'Don't be too harsh on her.'

Vaspine shifted his stare to Dodsley. 'And what makes one of my captives think he can tell me what to do with my own crew?'

'One of your captives who rescued you,' said Dodsley.

'It's true,' said Zoya, jumping between them. 'We wouldn't have been able to get here without him. And Eva.'

Eva stepped forward. Vaspine paused a moment, then nodded to them both. 'Thank you. There'll be time for introductions later. For now, we've got to move.' He walked over to Rosie, who'd moved further down the walkway to keep an eye on the stairs, still hugging Bucker. 'Rosie,' said Vaspine, 'I need you to get the crew somewhere safe, somewhere we can defend. Kane's men will be armed. We need to find somewhere to hold up while I think of a plan. Take them. Go!'

Zoya jumped forwards. 'On the way up here, I saw an armoury.' She pointed to the floor below. 'We can get weapons there.'

'OK,' said Vaspine to Rosie. 'Take the crew down, kit up and find a place to fight.'

'What are you going to do?'

'Just go.'

Rosie started to lead the crew along the walkway towards the stairs. A fire raged on the ground floor of the atrium now, its flames clawing the second level and starting to lick at the third. Waves of black smoke drifted up and pooled near the ceiling. Zoya, Dodsley, and Eva watched the others disappear through the fog, before Vaspine turned to them. 'Thank you for coming,' he said, 'but you too need to get out of here. Go on, follow them.'

Dodsley and Eva hesitated, then started to walk. Zoya remained. 'What are you going to do?'

'Zoya, go. That's an order.'

'You're going to fight him, aren't you?'

Vaspine nodded. 'It's time.'

'That's my fight, captain.' Zoya set her lips. 'You know that.'

'Not this time. Get out, while you can.'

'Too late, I'm afraid.' Zoya heard the voice behind her, cold and assured. She turned to see Lendon Kane standing at the edge of the walkway, one forearm locked around Eva's neck and the other holding a blade to her throat. 'I suggest you surrender, before I make a statement of intent with your friend here.'

Vaspine leapt forward, but he pulled up as Kane edged his knife closer to Eva's neck. 'I wouldn't come any closer,' he said.

'Let her go,' said Vaspine. 'It's me you want.'

Kane laughed. 'You? Oh no, Carlos, it's not just you. I want all of you. Every single one of you who destroyed my reputation.' He looked at Zoya. 'Especially the girl.'

'You can't have her,' said Vaspine.

'You don't have a choice this time,' said Kane. 'You're outnumbered. Your crew are already back under my control.' He glanced down at the second floor. 'Corridors are so easy to defend.'

Vaspine and Zoya followed his gaze, but it was too dark to see.

'I suggest you hand her to me and I'll ensure the rest of you have a painless death.'

Zoya glanced at the captain. 'Go and get everyone,' she said. 'I can handle this.'

'No!' snapped Vaspine.

'You have ten seconds,' said Kane.

'Please,' said Zoya, speaking to Vaspine. 'Please let me. This is my job. I was born for it. For my father, for Beebee, and everyone. Please let me.'

'Nine,' said Kane.

Dodsley approached the captain from behind and laid a hand on his shoulder. 'Go,' he said. 'A crew needs its captain. We've got this one.'

'Eight,' said Kane.

Vaspine regarded Dodsley, then the stairway behind him, and finally Zoya. 'You have to end it,' he said. 'No mercy.'

'I know,' said Zoya.

'Seven.'

Vaspine returned his gaze to Dodsley. 'I'll remember what you did today, thief.' With that, he sprinted towards the stairwell. Zoya and Dodsley watched him go.

'Six,' said Kane.

'Stop,' said Zoya. 'I'm here. And I'll give you the locket too. Just let her go.'

'What are you doing?' said Dodsley, his mouth open.

Zoya silenced him with a glare.

Kane smiled and loosened his grip on Eva's neck. 'Wise,' he said. 'Toss it over.'

Zoya reached up to her neck, unhooked her locket, closed it in her palm and tossed it at Kane's feet. 'Let her go,' said Zoya. 'You have what you want. You have the locket. And I'm right here. You don't need her any more.'

'I suppose not,' said Kane, as if the thought had never occurred. He smirked briefly, dragged Eva across the walkway, then shoved her over the edge of the rail and into the flames below.

43

Zoya dashed to the rail as Eva's body disappeared into the smoke. She stared into the dark and tried to pick out her friend, but it was no use. Eva was gone. From somewhere deep inside, Zoya felt a scream start to build until it erupted, so loud and long that the pain of it sent her to the floor. Over her shoulder, Dodsley growled as he drew his dagger and started to charge at Kane. The old man remained motionless until the younger was less than ten yards away, then lifted the dagger he'd held to Eva's neck, closed one eye and threw it. The blade travelled straight through the air, spinning end over end, before thudding deeply into Dodsley's thigh. The impact bent the thief in half and sent him tumbling to his right, where he slammed into the cell bars. His head made a sickening crack as it hit the metal, and he slumped to the floor.

Sensing the danger had passed, Kane took his handkerchief and used it to wipe down his suit. Satisfied, he slotted it back into his pocket and glanced down at the locket. 'You see,' he said, bending to pick it up, 'all I ever wanted was this little thing. If you'd have given it to me a year ago, we needn't have had any of this unpleasantness.'

Furious tears ran down Zoya's cheeks. She wiped them away with the back of her hand. 'And then what?' she murmured.

Kane cocked his head, trying to hear above the crackling flames. 'You're going to have to speak up,' he said. 'Didn't that orphanage owner teach you anything before I killed him?'

'Then what?' said Zoya, louder this time.

'What do you mean?' asked Kane, inspecting the pendant.

'Who's next?' said Zoya. She wiped another tear from her eyes. 'After us, who's next?'

'Whoever gets in my way. Whoever has what I want. I'm the greatest sky thief the world has ever seen. I didn't get rich robbing old ladies.'

'Then you'll never stop,' said Zoya. 'There'll always be something.'

Kane shrugged. 'Probably.' He started to walk towards the stairwell. Before he reached the first step, Zoya shouted from across the walkway.

'You're a coward.'

Kane stopped walking and turned around. Zoya pushed herself to her feet and shook her face free of tears. 'Only cowards take what they want.'

Kane started to walk back. 'What did you call me?'

'You heard me,' said Zoya.

A snarl tore across Kane's face. 'You contemptible child. You have the temerity to call *me* a coward?'

'You are,' said Zoya, her voice growing in strength. 'Only cowards kill to get what they want. My mother and father didn't kill. Vaspine doesn't kill. Beebee didn't kill. Eva didn't kill.' She glanced at Dodsley's silent form. 'Dodsley didn't. Mr Whycherley didn't. You have killed so many of the people I love.'

'And now I'm going to kill you,' snapped Kane.

Zoya staggered to the centre of the walkway. 'You can't. I've beaten you once and I'll beat you again.'

Kane glared, then shook his head, removed his jacket and threw it to the floor. He drew another dagger and started to advance. 'I'm going to enjoy this.'

Zoya was taken aback at the speed of Kane's approach, and she stumbled back to the rail. As the pirate closed in, she fumbled to draw her sword—gripping the handle tight and pulling hard. The blade wouldn't move. Zoya glanced up just in time to see Kane, teeth bared, swing his dagger in an arcing loop. She leapt back. Kane followed, and swung again. This time, Zoya darted under his free arm and scudded along the walkway. As she moved, she wrestled again with the hilt of her sword and this time it came away. But the momentum of the movement threw her to the left and she only just managed to stand in time to parry another blow from Kane, then another, as he rained swipes on her, slashing and cutting.

Zoya used everything she'd learned about sword-fighting now, ducking under Kane's arm as he tried to crash it down, rolling by his side when his back was turned and sliding under his legs as he raised his dagger to slash at her face. Kane was quick, and he spun as Zoya slid beneath him and advanced again, backing her up against the rail. Zoya glanced quickly into the atrium. The flames had reached the top floor now, and were starting to singe the walkway.

'It would be fitting if I killed you like I killed your friend,' said Kane, nodding down into the flames.

Zoya searched desperately for a way out, but Kane's stance was so wide she couldn't get past. The only way was to leap over the rail. This she did, landing with her feet on a slim metal support that ran parallel to the walkway. Her left foot buckled as she landed, then slipped, sending her sword spinning into the flames below and forcing her to grip the upper rail with her hands. Kane started to stab at her knuckles with his dagger— quick, jabbing thrusts. Zoya hopped from foot to foot, twisting her body and shifting her hands to avoid the blade. After a few seconds, Kane became frustrated and pulled back ready to lurch over the bar. Sensing her chance, Zoya swung along the rail, out of Kane's reach. As she moved, his blade nicked her ear, causing a hot line of blood to run down her neck. Zoya ignored the cut and continued along the rail. Only once she'd put a dozen yards between her and Kane did she boost herself back over and land on the walkway.

The platform was burning now, so that Zoya had to hop to avoid the flames. Desperate for a weapon, she searched the platform around her but there was nothing nearby. She glanced up at Kane, who bore down on her again. Something in the picture jogged Zoya's memory, and suddenly everything around her seemed to slow. A rush of images flashed past her mind—Mr Whycherley, Beebee, Eva, Dodsley, Vaspine. She heard a voice ringing in her ears, one she hadn't heard for a year. 'You've got to fight the nasty ones,' it said. 'If you don't, no-one will.'

Beebee's words sent a charge through Zoya. She took a breath, then sprinted at Kane as fast as she could. She clattered into his stomach, Kane's dagger narrowly missing the back of her neck. Digging her feet into the wood, she drove him backwards, cracking his head on an unseen metal crossbeam. As he fell, she threw herself down on him— spilling his dagger across the walkway. Kane kicked his legs a couple of times, then recovered and threw Zoya into the air to get her away. As she landed, he catapulted himself to his feet and started to advance again.

Across the walkway, Zoya rose groggily, a loud ringing in her ears. She shook her head to clear the sound, but it remained. Kane followed her as she backed away, moving quicker with every step. Behind her, Zoya heard a loud crack.

As she turned, a large section of the walkway disintegrated into the flames. The collapse created a gap in the platform that ran its whole width. Without thinking, Zoya ran at the gap as fast as she could. However, with just a yard to go she realized the jump was too far and pulled up short, her foot skidding so close to the edge that she had to throw her entire weight back towards Kane to stop herself from falling. When she managed to right herself, Kane had caught her.

He peered into the hole and smirked. 'Remind you of anything?'

Zoya didn't respond.

'You know,' continued Kane, 'when you managed to throw me off that airship, I had to say I was quite impressed. You and your little friends really were the fly in my honey for a while.' He laughed. 'I sometimes thought, when I was rebuilding my crew, that I might ask you to join us. You'd have made a good sky thief. You remind me of me when I was younger.'

'I'm nothing like you!' said Zoya.

'I know,' said Kane. 'I realized that. And since that moment, your fate has only ever pointed in one direction. Right here, to the edge of your doom. I have the locket, and now I will have my revenge. I'm going to enjoy killing you.'

Kane started to advance. Instead of screaming, or trying to leap to safety, Zoya smiled. It was a cool smile, a knowing smile. And it made Kane pause. 'Your death amuses you?'

Zoya shook her head.

Kane narrowed his eyebrows. 'What?'

'The locket.'

Kane looked down towards his pocket, where he'd deposited the jewellery. As he did, Zoya reached under her shirt and pulled out the chain that was still hanging there. She unclipped it and held it in her fist. 'It's here.'

Kane stared at Zoya. When her expression did not change, he backed up a little and took out the locket she'd thrown earlier. Holding the pendant up to the flames, he peered at it, then at the one on Zoya's chain. They were similar at a glance, but even in the smoke it was clear which was Jupiter's. Kane flung his locket away.

Without warning, he charged. A jolt of panic surged through Zoya, and she tossed Jupiter's locket up in the air. Kane's eyes followed the chain, and he shifted his body to intercept it. Zoya slipped past him, spinning so she landed facing the pirate. The locket hung in the air at the top of its arc, its chain whipping at clouds of smoke, before it started to drop over the gap. Kane leapt to catch it, diving onto his belly and sliding along the wooden boards. He managed to close his fingers around the locket just as it was moving beyond his reach, and somehow throw himself to safety.

Zoya felt her stomach lurch as he rolled onto his back and began to push himself upright. However, as he did, a smouldering crack appeared in the wood near his feet and the panel on which he stood started to crumble. Kane's eyes flew open when he realized what was happening, and he kicked his legs frantically, trying to get back up. But it was no use. Another loud crack, and then a tearing sound, and finally the panel tore and fell away.

Zoya watched Lendon Kane vanish, with her locket, into the roaring fire below.

44

Zoya lay on her back in the dark, her breathing heavy and pulse pounding. She wanted to push herself up, to crawl to the gap and check Kane was really gone. But every time she tried to manoeuvre onto her elbows, her arms gave way and she dropped back to the walkway. After a couple of attempts, Zoya gave up and allowed her head to roll back so it was resting on the wood. She watched the smoke collect beneath the ceiling and felt at peace. She imagined herself back on the *Dragonfly*, lying on the deck under the sun, sliding between a world of wakefulness and dreams. On the walkway, she breathed in deep lungfuls of black smoke. And like her daydream, she started to slide from consciousness.

A few seconds passed.

A few more.

Then came a voice. 'You going to help me?'

Zoya heard the sound as if it was far away. She tried

268

to gather the energy to respond, but when she moved her mouth no sound emerged.

'Oi!' came the voice again, more insistent this time. 'Come and help me!'

Zoya opened her eyes and blinked away the stinging smoke. The voice was coming from behind her. She pushed herself up and craned her head. Propped up against the cell bars was Dodsley Brown. Kane's dagger protruded out of his right leg.

'You might want to sleep in this barbecue,' said Dodsley, raising his head, 'but I don't.'

Zoya smiled, then rolled onto her hands and knees and started to crawl over.

'You need to get this knife out of me,' said Dodsley when she arrived.

'Now?'

'It's either now and we can get out of this fire, or we do it when I'm in heaven.'

Zoya looked at the dagger.

'First,' said Dodsley, 'rip off a bit of my shirt.'

Zoya did as she was told, tearing a strip of fabric from what remained of his shirt.

'Now, I want you to take the handle,' he said, teeth gritted with pain. 'When I say pull, pull back as hard as you can. Yes?'

'OK,' said Zoya.

269

'Pull.'

Zoya leaned forwards, wrapped her hands around the knife, and yanked as hard as she could. The blade left Dodsley's leg in one smooth movement. As soon as she had it out, she tossed it behind her and over the edge of the walkway. In the meantime, Dodsley had tied the shirt around the wound and was applying pressure with both hands.

'Right, we need to go and get Eva.' He pushed himself to his feet, wincing as he moved.

Zoya put a hand on his arm. 'She's dead.'

'No. We saw her fall, that's all. She might still be alive.'

'It's fifty feet.'

Dodsley grabbed her shoulders. 'Would she leave you?'

Zoya shook her head.

'Then let's go.'

Zoya nodded.

Together, they searched the walkway for a way down. The smoke was so thick now that Zoya struggled to see the bottom of the atrium. She stumbled to the gap through which Kane had fallen, but it was too far for them to jump, especially with Dodsley's leg. Dodsley checked the stairwell. 'No good,' he said, 'it's broken away. We're going to have to climb down the walkway.'

'The outside?' said Zoya, bug-eyed. 'What about your leg?'

'You got a better idea?'

She didn't. To avoid the worst of the smoke, they made

their way to the opposite corner of the prison and peered over the edge of the walkway. The level below was about ten feet down.

'I'll go first, you follow,' said Dodsley.

Dodsley descended so that he was hanging from his arms, then started to swing until his body was positioned above the lower walkway. When he was happy he'd land safely, he let go. 'OK,' he said, his voice cracking with pain, 'it works. Go!'

Zoya took a breath, stepped back off the walkway, and hung down. As Dodsley had a moment before, she swung until her momentum took her over the lower level, then she let go. She landed a yard from Dodsley, her body jolting on the metal.

Once they'd righted themselves, Zoya led him over to the edge for their next jump. 'Same again?'

Dodsley nodded. Zoya shouldered him back so she could go first this time, jumping quickly over the rail and down to the ground. She nodded for Dodsley to follow, and positioned herself so she could catch him if he stumbled. Dodsley came down with a thud, his weight landing entirely on his injured leg. His face contorted as a lance of pain shot up his thigh. He stood with his eyes closed and his jaw locked, waiting for it to pass.

Fire covered the entire ground floor now—orange flames as tall as Zoya. The heat seared her, so she had to shield her face to stop it from burning. She peered through parted fingers while she waited for Dodsley to recover, trying to find Eva.

'Where did she fall?' asked Dodsley.

'I didn't see.'

Dodsley let out a growl and started searching for a shape amongst the flames. Zoya did the same, and spotted Eva a moment later——her body lying on the other side of a wall of flames. She pointed it out to Dodsley, who started to hobble in that direction, holding up his forearm to shield his face. Zoya followed. They cut through the flames to find Eva lying on her back, arms spread and legs crossed, her face blackened. Fighting tears, Zoya collapsed by her side and put her ear to Eva's mouth. She waited a second, then another.

Nothing.

Zoya's heart sank. Above her, Dodsley waited, his body rigid. Zoya glanced up, profound sadness in her eyes. Dodsley read the look and turned away, dropping to his knees. Zoya watched him, then opened her mouth to speak, to say something. But before she could, she felt a small puff of air on her cheek. Immediately, she looked down at Eva.

Eva's eyelashes flickered.

'Dodsley,' said Zoya, her eyes lighting up, 'quick!'

Dodsley looked up slowly. When he saw Eva shift slightly, a large smile took over his face and he leapt to his feet. He limped across and gathered her up in his arms. Eva opened her eyes, glanced briefly at Dodsley, smiled, then closed them again and dropped her head.

'Where's the way out?' snapped Dodsley.

Zoya peered through the flames, searching for the narrow sliver of light that marked the front doors. She found it—a vertical crack about twenty yards behind them. She ran over and tried to open the doors, but they wouldn't budge. Frustrated, she leapt back, then threw her entire weight at the doors, but they bounced her back as if she were a pebble. Dodsley had caught up with her now, and was standing behind with Eva in his arms.

'They won't open,' she said.

'Kick them,' shouted Dodsley.

Zoya looked at the doors, backed up, planted her left foot and drove her right boot at the point where the two doors met. The wood moved an inch or so, but held. Nevertheless, Zoya had widened the sliver of light a tiny amount, and it gave her hope. She felt a breeze now, blowing through the gap.

'Again!' shouted Dodsley.

Zoya sent her boot into the doors once more. This time, they swung open, spilling Zoya onto the ground. Dodsley followed, staggering into the courtyard for a few yards, then dropping to his knees, with Eva tumbling to the floor. Zoya glanced at the pair to check they were OK, then collapsed onto her back.

It was so bright in the sun that she had to close her eyes, and she breathed in big lungfuls of fresh, clean air. After thirty seconds, she started to breathe normally again, and she opened her eyes. Above, a silhouetted figure blocked out the sun. It was a man, standing with his hands on his hips and a sword strapped to his side. Surrounding him were half a dozen others, each staring at her. Zoya surveyed them, then looked again at the first. His silhouette was one she'd have recognized anywhere. She sat up and shielded her eyes so she could see his face.

'Hello captain,' she said.

45

Minutes passed before Zoya made a move to lift herself off the floor. When she did, a number of the crew rushed over to help her, but she pushed them away. She took a moment to steady herself, then managed to stand without falling. Around her lay a scene of devastation. There were about thirty sky thieves in all—most of the crew of the *Dragonfly*—standing or sitting in twos and threes, their faces blackened and bodies bruised. Behind them, the prison still burned ferociously—a thick column of smoke rising from its roof. In the courtyard lay the wreckage of the *Ocean's Doom*, and beside that, tied together, were a dozen of Kane's men. They looked furious, staring enviously at a pile of nearby weapons. Guarding them was Rosie, with her arm around Bucker, and a few other sky thieves.

Zoya searched for Vaspine, saluted to show she was OK, then made her way over to Dodsley and Eva, who were receiving treatment from the Doc.

She caught Dodsley's eye, then glanced down at Eva. 'Is she all right?'

'I'm fine,' said Eva. 'Just remind me never to do you a favour again.'

Zoya chuckled.

'He's not doing so good, though,' continued Eva, nodding at Dodsley. She looked at the Doc. 'This nice man says he's going to have to chop off his leg.'

Zoya's mouth dropped open, then she caught a smirk on the Doc's face and realized it was a joke.

'He'll be fine,' said the Doc. He finished winding a fresh strip of fabric around Dodsley's leg and moved onto another injured pirate nearby.

'Listen,' said Zoya, avoiding their eyes. 'I just wanted to say thank you. Both of you. You didn't have to come here. You didn't have to go anywhere. So, thanks.'

Eva shrugged. 'That's what friends are for.'

Zoya smiled.

Eva elbowed Dodsley in the ribs. Startled, he looked across, then understood. 'No trouble,' he said, turning back to Zoya. 'It was nice to do something good for once. I don't know,' he looked up to the sky, grinning mischievously, 'maybe it's worth a reward. I really did like those goggles . . .'

Eva elbowed him again.

'OK, maybe not,' said Dodsley.

'If anyone should be thanking anyone,' said Vaspine,

crossing the courtyard, 'it should be me thanking all of you. Bucker, too. I'll never know why you risked your lives to come and get us. But I'm glad you did.'

Zoya frowned. 'I lost the locket, captain,' she said. 'Kane fell with it into the fire.'

Vaspine reached a hand into his pocket. He brought out Zoya's necklace and held it before her, its pendant swinging from the end of its chain. Zoya chuckled, amazed, then extended a hand for him to throw it over. When he did, Zoya hooked the locket around her neck. After a moment, she looked up. 'Did I get him?'

'He's gone,' said Vaspine. 'I saw the body myself.' The captain smiled, then bowed to the others and walked towards Charlie, who was nursing a gashed cheek nearby. Before he'd made it more than a few yards, he turned back and looked at Zoya. 'Did I mention to you we were looking for a couple of new sky thieves to join the crew?' Vaspine feigned a pondering face, as if considering the problem. 'Zoya, if you think of anyone, let me know.'

Zoya smiled, then looked at Dodsley and Eva. The pair smiled back.

'They say yes!' said Zoya to Vaspine.

'Good,' said the captain, nodding absent-mindedly.

Vaspine walked off towards Charlie. Zoya stayed with Dodsley and Eva a few minutes longer, telling them what happened in the prison, all about her fight with Kane, and

Eva's rescue. When she was done, she gave each of them a hug goodbye, then headed off towards Cid. The pilot was lying on his back on the ground, his head wedged up against a chunk of the *Ocean's Doom*. He glanced up at Zoya. 'Here's a hero if ever I saw one. How are you doing, kiddo?'

'I'm fine,' said Zoya, twirling on the spot. 'How are you? All the way here, I was worried you were dead. When Kane shot you . . .'

'A scratch,' said Cid, dismissing it with a wave of his hand. He shifted his gaze to the other injured thieves. His face darkened. 'Did you get him?'

'I got him,' said Zoya.

Cid nodded. 'That's my girl. Hopefully he won't be back this time.'

Zoya glanced down at the pilot. His face was pale and he had big, black rings under his eyes. Zoya had never seen him look so old. She sank down next to him and held his hand. 'Are you going to be OK?'

'I'll be fine,' said Cid. 'Doc says as soon as we get to the surface, he'll get the bullet out. It hasn't hit anything vital. I'll have a scar though.'

Zoya chuckled. 'Beebee would have been proud.'

'Yeah,' said Cid, smiling at the thought. 'Yes, he would.' The pilot let the memory of his friend linger, then jerked his thumb over his shoulder. 'You should go and see Rosie. She'll want to know you got him.'

Zoya glanced over his shoulder, where Rosie was still guarding Kane's men. Pushing herself to her feet, Zoya smiled a goodbye then wandered through the clumps of sky thieves towards her friend. When Rosie saw her, she pulled them all together for a hug. 'You can't imagine how good it is to see you,' said Rosie. 'We were all so worried.'

'You were?' said Zoya. 'We were worried about you guys. We didn't even know where you were!'

Rosie laughed, then pushed her away to get a proper look. 'You look all right,' she said. 'you must have fought well. Not many swordfighters can keep Kane at bay for long. I guess all those hours of training paid off.'

'Yeah,' said Zoya, thinking back. 'I guess they did.'

Zoya's head was hurting now—a dull ache behind her left eye—and she searched the courtyard for somewhere to sit alone. Spotting the *Ocean's Doom*'s upturned oil engine embedded in the earth a short distance from the main wreckage, she made her way over and sat on the cold metal. She ran her hands along the surface to cool herself down.

'Room for one more?'

Zoya looked up to see Bucker framed by the sun. He looked tired. 'Of course,' she said. 'Sit down.'

Bucker hauled himself onto the engine, then twisted around so that his legs dangled above the ground. 'I can't believe we did it,' he said, kicking off his shoes. 'I don't know how.'

Zoya shrugged. 'Some bravery. A bit of luck.'

'And some help,' said Bucker, nodding at Dodsley and Eva. 'We couldn't have done it without them.'

'No,' said Zoya. She rubbed her eyes. 'You know, they just agreed to join the crew? The captain invited them.'

When he realized she was being serious, Bucker smiled. 'That's . . . awesome.'

'Yeah.'

A small bird glided down from the sky and landed in the dust next to the engine. It eyed them warily, then started to peck at a couple of tomatoes that had spilled from the airship's galley. Zoya and Bucker watched as it ate.

'What are we going to do?' asked Bucker, eventually.

'What do you mean?'

'Now,' said Bucker. 'What are we going to do? Mum said we lost some of the crew. And we haven't got a ship, no coins, clothes, nothing.'

'We'll be all right,' said Zoya. 'We always are.'

'Maybe not this time.' Bucker frowned. 'We're stuck here.'

Zoya thought about what he'd said and realized he was right. They were stuck. Stuck thousands of feet up on an island in the sky. Their ship had gone. Their gold had gone, their weapons, everything they needed to be a real sky thief crew. And yet, Zoya was determined to fight off despair. She hadn't travelled all the way from the forest, down the cliff, through the village, over the Titan, up into Dalmacia, stolen the airship or fought Lendon Kane to lie down and die.

An idea formed in her head. Kane was a sky thief—not their kind, but still a thief. He was also a captain. That meant he must have an airship.

She jumped down off the engine, startling the bird, which fluttered away. 'We're not stuck,' she said to Bucker. 'We're not stuck at all. Come on.'

Bucker slid down and followed Zoya as she circled the courtyard. Eventually, she found what she was looking for and led him through a maze of buildings until they came across one that was bigger than the rest. It was a corrugated metal square with a curved roof, jutting out of which was a tall, wooden pole. Drooping off the pole were two white ropes. 'That's it,' said Zoya.

'That's what?' said Bucker.

Zoya rolled her eyes and sprinted off towards the double doors at the front of the building. The doors swung open easily when she pulled the iron handles, nearly knocking her to the floor. She had just about regained her balance when Bucker jogged up behind. She gestured for him to go inside, then followed. For a minute, they picked their way through an entrance hallway full of paint cans, brushes, and overalls, then ducked under an archway and emerged into the main body of the building. As they passed beneath the arch, Zoya darted ahead and spun around so she could see the look on Bucker's face.

When he realized what he was seeing, his mouth dropped open. 'Whoa.'

'Yep,' said Zoya.

'How did you know it was here?'

Zoya laughed. 'I didn't. Call it a hunch.'

Ahead of them stood an enormous airship—a huge, black behemoth with dual central masts and a massive oil engine attached to the stern. The craft was anchored to the ground by a network of wide, leather straps and it was held upright by wooden crossbeams, so they could see little of the deck that lay fifty yards above their heads. Instead, their view was filled with the curved wood of the hull, painted black.

Bucker had wandered further into the hangar now, and he ran his hand along the bottom of the ship. 'We'd have to paint it,' he said. 'And I'm sure the captain will want to give it a clean.'

'That's OK,' said Zoya. 'We could start now.' She bolted back through the arch and returned with a brush and a tin of paint. She dropped the tin to the floor, dunked the brush inside and started to daub on the side of the airship. Bucker watched her, trying to work out what she was doing. After a few letters he understood, and nipped to get a brush of his own. A few minutes later, they laid down their brushes and stepped back to admire their work.

Huge letters on the side of the airship now read, *Dragonfly II*.

'It's got a nice ring to it,' said Zoya.

'Agreed,' said Bucker.

Zoya turned to her friend and saluted. 'Lookout-boy, please go and fetch the captain. Tell him we've found him a new airship.'

Bucker stamped his foot and returned the salute. 'Aye ma'am.' He laughed. 'Right away.'

Zoya watched Bucker duck under the arch, then looked back at the ship.

It wasn't the original *Dragonfly*, and it never would be. All those memories could only live in her mind now. No, this was something new, a source of hope. Zoya smiled to herself, happy at what she'd accomplished. She felt like she'd won her family back, and it sent a wave of warmth through her. She began to climb the criss-cross of leather straps and wooden beams, clambering along the hull, up over the gunwale and onto the deck of her new home.

DAN WALKER

Dan Walker, 32, lives smack-bang in the centre of the UK, just outside of a city called Nottingham, with his lovely, patient, and supportive partner Dominika.

Dan spent his childhood being dragged up and down the hills of the Peak District, frantically hammering away at computer games, and raiding his cousin's bookshelf for anything with a colourful cover. He later tricked the University of Derby into allowing him admission, before graduating with a First-Class degree in English. Since then, he has worked with a procession of wonderful people in bookshops, libraries, and schools. He currently helps to run a specialist Autism centre.

On the rare occasion you find Dan away from the computer, he can be found trying to tease a melodious sound out of his guitar, re-reading his favourite books for the eighty-eighth time, or fighting off everyone nearby for the last blueberry in the pack.